The voice on the phone . . .

"I hate Call Waiting," Karen said. "It always interrupts at the wrong time. Hold on a sec, okay?"

"Okay," Ethan agreed.

More clicks. Then silence.

When Karen returned to Ethan a few seconds later, her voice was trembling and weak. "Ethan, please — come over! Come over here right away!"

"Karen? What's wrong?" Ethan demanded.

"The voice on the phone. It was so *horrible*, Ethan. He said he was going to kill me!"

Don't miss these other thrillers
by R.L. Stine:

The Baby-sitter
The Baby-sitter II
The Baby-sitter III
The Boyfriend
The Girlfriend
The Dead Girlfriend
Blind Date
Halloween Night
Hit and Run
The Hitchhiker
Twisted
Beach House
The Snowman
Beach Party

R.L.STINE

SCHOLASTIC INC.
New York Toronto London Auckland Sydney

No part of this publication may be reproduced in whole or in part, or stored in a retrieval system, or transmitted in any form or by any means, electronic, mechanical, photocopying, recording, or otherwise, without written permission of the publisher. For information regarding permission, write to Scholastic Inc., 555 Broadway, New York 10012.

ISBN 0-590-47480-4

Copyright © 1994 by Robert L. Stine. All rights reserved. Published by Scholastic Inc.

12 11 10 9 8 7 6 5 4 3 2 1   4 5 6 7 8 9/9

Printed in the U.S.A.   01

First Scholastic printing, February 1994

Chapter 1

The frightening phone calls began less than an hour after Karen had the fight with Ethan.

One week before the fight, on a snowy, bone-chilling Saturday night, Karen Masters pulled her blue Corolla onto Jefferson, Ethan's street. The tires crunched over the salted pavement as Karen eased to the curb and cut the headlights.

She reached to turn the ignition key, but her friend Micah Davis grabbed her arm to stop her. "Karen, if you turn off the engine, we won't have any heat. We'll freeze."

Karen stared thoughtfully out the windshield, past the clicking wipers at the falling snow. "I know," she said. "But I'm nearly out of gas. If we have to wait a long time . . ."

Micah unlatched the seat belt so she could turn to Karen. "This is so crazy. I don't know what you hope to see," she said, shaking her head.

In the shadowy light, Karen caught Micah's disapproving frown. The wipers scraped across the windshield. The snowflakes were large and wet. Before they were brushed away, the light from the streetlamp made them glisten like teardrops.

"I don't know, either," Karen sighed, resting both gloved hands on the wheel.

"It's a rotten night for spying," Micah complained in a velvety voice. She tossed her blonde hair behind her shoulders. Then she ducked her head lower into the collar of her down coat. "I mean it. This is really crazy, Karen."

"I know," Karen agreed. "I just have to see . . ." Her voice trailed off.

"See what?" Micah demanded.

"I have to see if Ethan lied to me," Karen said. She turned off the engine. The wipers stopped halfway across their route, then slid into place."Good. Silence. I can't stand that *click-click-click!*" she exclaimed.

"You're a nervous nut," Micah accused. "You've been a nervous nut for days."

"It's all Ethan's fault," Karen insisted. Her dark eyes stared straight ahead. She had parked at the top of the low, sloping hill that led down to Ethan Parker's house.

From this spot, she could see the Parkers' sprawling redwood ranch-style house and the short driveway that led to the garage at the side. A spotlight over the front door cast a bright rectangle of light over the snow-covered front lawn.

"Look at you," Micah said sharply, grabbing the sleeve of Karen's bulky sweater. "You're so pale, Karen. And you look positively anorexic."

"It's dark. How can you see if I'm pale or not?" Karen replied shrilly, tugging her sleeve free. "And I'm not anorexic. Everyone in my family is very thin."

She pulled off her wool ski cap and shook her short, dark hair free. And then she added pointedly, "Especially since we don't gobble down Kit Kat bars every minute."

Micah had a serious Kit Kat problem.

"Wish I had one now," Micah muttered. She gazed out at the falling snow. "I can't believe I agreed to come with you tonight!" she exclaimed.

Micah pushed her hair back with both hands. She had piles of curly blonde hair, and she was constantly playing with it, pushing at it, tugging at strands, twirling them around her fingers.

She shivered. "What do you think we're

going to see, Karen — before they find us frozen solid inside this car?"

"Ethan broke our date tonight," Karen replied, her voice revealing her emotion. She crossed her arms in front of her chest. "I want to see if he lied to me. I want to see what time he gets home."

"What's that going to prove?" Micah demanded. "If he gets home after midnight, is that going to prove he was out with Wendy Talbot?"

Karen started to reply, but the windshield suddenly glowed brightly. Headlights from behind them. An approaching car.

"Maybe that's him!" Karen whispered.

Both girls slid down low in their seats.

The bright lights rolled over the windshield. The car, a dark Taurus wagon, rumbled past them and kept going, moving slowly over the snow-slick street.

"False alarm," Karen said. She glanced at the dashboard clock, but it was a blank because the engine was off.

Micah sat up and tapped her long fingernails on the door. "You know, just because you saw him talking to Wendy in the hall after school doesn't mean they have a date or anything."

"I *told* you," Karen replied sharply. "It was the *way* he was talking to her. He was leaning over her. And when they laughed, she put her hand on his shoulder. Like she *owned* him or something."

"Karen — really!"

"Okay, okay," Karen muttered. "Not like she owned him. But she was definitely coming on to him. And he was loving it."

"So? Wendy is a flirt," Micah said, shrugging. "Everyone knows that. What does *that* prove?"

"Why are you defending her?" Karen demanded.

She immediately thought: Of *course* Micah would defend Wendy. Micah is a flirt, too. Micah is always coming on to boys, putting her hand on their arm as they talk. Micah always stands really close to boys, so close it makes them uncomfortable. And she's always purring at them with that sexy voice she has.

Micah is just like Wendy, Karen thought.

And then she scolded herself for thinking such cruel thoughts. Micah is my best friend, after all, Karen reminded herself. Micah is always there for me. She's here for me right now.

"I'm not defending Wendy," Micah insisted patiently. "I'm just trying to prove to you that you're crazy!" She laughed. "I mean, what are friends for?"

Karen didn't join in the laughter. "Don't you understand, Micah? This is the first Saturday that Ethan and I haven't been together."

"Karen — "

"The same day I saw him drooling all over Wendy Talbot in school, he called me and said he had to work the late shift at the Sizzler and couldn't see me Saturday night. Am I supposed to believe that?"

"Yes," Micah replied quickly. "Listen, Karen, you've got to stop acting so jealous. Really."

"If Ethan broke up with me — " Karen started. But the words caught in her throat. She couldn't bear to think about it.

"Oh, it's so *cold* in here!" Micah complained with a loud groan. "Feel my nose. Go ahead. Feel it. It's totally frozen, Karen."

"I can't feel your nose. I'm wearing gloves," Karen told her.

"Ethan isn't going to break up with you to start going with Wendy Talbot," Micah assured her. "But even if he does, Karen — "

She grabbed Karen's sleeve. "Even if he does, it isn't the end of the world, you know? I mean, really. There are lots of other guys. You can't go totally to pieces — even *if* Ethan is interested in someone else."

Karen's dark eyes flashed. "You know

something — don't you!" she accused shrilly. "You know something about Ethan and Wendy, and you're not telling me!"

"No way!" Micah cried. "No way. I don't know anything. I'm just trying to help you. You know. I'm trying to give you a reality check, Karen. You're pretty. You're smart. Even if Ethan dumps you, you won't have any trouble — "

"Stop it!" Karen snapped, her voice trembling. "I don't want to talk about it."

Micah lowered her eyes and fiddled with the charm bracelet on her wrist. "Sorry," she murmured.

"No, *I'm* sorry," Karen replied quickly. "You're right, Micah. I'm a nervous nut. I didn't mean to snap at you. You're a true friend for coming along with me tonight. Really."

Micah traced her finger along the clouded-up passenger window. "Well, I just don't get it," she said softly. "I mean, if you think Ethan is out with Wendy, why aren't we parked in front of Wendy's house?"

"I don't want to see them together," Karen replied. "I really don't. I just want to see what time Ethan gets home."

Micah rubbed her hand in a wide circle on the passenger window, trying to make a peephole. "We can't see *anything* now!" she complained. "The windows are covered with snow, Karen. It's like being inside an igloo."

Karen only heard part of what her friend was saying. She had drifted into her unhappy thoughts. Once again, she pictured Ethan parked somewhere with Wendy. She pictured his arm around Wendy. She imagined them snuggling close, kissing, while the snow floated down over Ethan's car.

"You didn't hear a word I said," Micah accused, tapping Karen several times on the shoulder of her sweater. "Hey — snap out of it."

"Oh. Sorry." Karen glanced around. "I'd better scrape the windshield. I didn't realize."

She popped the trunk, pushed open the car door, pulled on her wool cap, and was immediately greeted by a blast of cold air and wet snowflakes. "I have a scraper in the trunk," she told Micah.

"Close the door!" Micah screamed. "It must be twenty below!"

Karen started toward the trunk, her boots crunching over the soft snow that blanketed the street.

The wet snowflakes tickled her face.

Soft as a kiss, she thought dreamily.

Ethan, where are you?

Leaning against the trunk, she gazed down

the hill to his house. The bright spotlight on the front of the house caught the falling snow, making the flakes white againt the low, purple sky. The slanted roof was blanketed with snow. The windows were all dark.

Sighing, Karen pulled up the trunk lid.

As the tiny trunk light came on, the boy's body came slowly into view.

The body was folded neatly in the trunk, the arms tucked underneath.

From out of the deep shadows, the boy's lifeless eyes stared up at Karen.

Karen opened her mouth to scream, but no sound came out.

Chapter 2

A low, terrified moan escaped Karen's throat.

In the dim light, the body in the trunk appeared to shift.

Or was that her imagination?

"Micah — help me!" Her cry came out a whisper, blown back in her face by a wet gust of wind.

And then Karen recognized the body.

A dummy. A mannequin.

The dumb department store mannequin her brother, Chris, had found years ago in a trash dump and had carrried home to keep in his room.

Karen uttered an angry cry. She grabbed the plastic scraper and slammed the trunk lid shut, bouncing the car.

Chris and his stupid practical jokes!

He knew the mannequin would scare her to

death. Especially in the stressed-out state she'd been in.

Why did Chris think it was such a riot to frighten her?

He was older, bigger, smarter. He was already in college. He had a million friends and lots of girlfriends. So why did he have to prove how superior he was with all the dumb practical jokes he was always pulling?

I'll pay him back, Karen thought. I'll find a way to get him.

She slipped as she headed toward the windshield. Her feet started to slide out from under her, and she stumbled forward onto the hood of the car.

Pushing herself up with both hands, she quickly brushed the wet snow off the front of her sweater. Then she began scraping the windshield.

She felt cold droplets of snow in her hair that poked out from under the wool cap. Snowflakes clung to her eyelashes, making her blink as she worked to clear the windshield. Even three layers of sweaters couldn't keep out the cold.

Micah is right. This really is crazy, Karen thought.

We should have rented a movie and stayed in the nice, warm house.

But I couldn't, Karen realized. I couldn't just sit home thinking Ethan had lied to me, wondering where he was, wondering what he was doing — and with whom.

As she scraped the passenger side, Micah came into view. She was huddled low on the seat, staring out questioningly at Karen, her head buried in her coat collar, her hands shoved into her coat pockets.

I really took Ethan for granted, Karen thought, up until tonight. I guess I didn't realize how much he means to me until now. My life was really empty until Ethan and I started going together last year.

Karen and Micah had only been friends since the start of the school year. Before Ethan, Karen had spent a lot of lonely time. Her parents had had an angry divorce three years before. Karen's father had left home without even saying good-bye to her.

Karen had always had an intense personality. She took things seriously. She was always trying to figure out what people really meant by the things they said or did.

Her mother seemed to take the divorce better than Karen did. Karen had received only two letters from her father in three years.

Now the house was empty most of the time. Mrs. Masters had to work long hours at the department store where she was a floor manager. And Karen's big brother, Chris, was always busy with his college friends.

Ethan had saved Karen from her loneliness.

He was good for her. He was funny and outgoing and playful. He knew how to have fun. He kept her from getting too serious, too intense.

They took long bike rides along the river. They loved to ride to the high peak that overlooked town and gaze down at the tiny houses and shops below them.

They both loved trivia games. They played Trivial Pursuit until the cards were ragged and bent. Karen taught Ethan chess. They both enjoyed quiet, rainy evenings, staring at each other over the chessboard.

So many good times they had shared.

They had become so close, so close. . . .

But tonight he had dumped her for Wendy Talbot.

Karen knew he had. She just knew it.

And here she was, in the middle of a snowstorm, parked on the hill above his house, waiting — waiting for *what*?

Suddenly, the driver's window slid down, startling Karen from her thoughts. Micah, leaning over the seat, poked her head out.

"Hey — you don't have to scrape off the glass!"

"Oh. Yeah. Right." Karen hadn't realized the windshield was nearly cleared.

"Get in!" Micah called.

Karen obediently climbed in behind the wheel, quickly pulling the door shut. She dropped the scraper onto the floor beside Micah. "Ooh. I can't stop shivering," she said, brushing snow off her wool cap. "I have to turn on the heat. If we run out of gas — "

"I have an idea," Micah interrupted. "Let's drive to the Sizzler."

"Huh?" Karen hugged herself, trying to warm up. She was breathing hard, and her breath was steaming up the windshield.

"Drive to the Sizzler," Micah repeated. "If you see that Ethan is hard at work there, you'll feel better. Then we'll go to my house and make a fire, and try to warm up."

"But — but — " Karen hesitated, her mind spinning. "What if Ethan sees me? He'll know I was spying on him. Or . . . what if he isn't there, Micah? Really. I couldn't *stand* it if he wasn't there. I — "

"Karen, do you want to know the truth or not?" Micah demanded.

Karen couldn't reply. She wasn't sure *what* she wanted to know. "Maybe we should just go home," she muttered unhappily.

Micah started to reply, but bright lights against the windshield made her stop.

Both girls ducked low as white headlights shone through the car. A car roared past, speeding over the snow-covered street, down the hill.

At the bottom of the hill, its brakelights went on, and the car slid wildly, spun all the way around, then swerved into the Parkers' driveway. "It's him," Karen murmured, immediately recognizing Ethan's red Bonneville.

"Does he always drive like that?" Micah demanded, rolling her eyes.

"*Ssshhh,*" Karen whispered. Through the snow-dotted windshield, she could see Ethan climb out of his car and jog through the bright rectangle of light to his front door.

"Can we go now?" Micah whispered. "You saw him. You didn't prove anything. But you saw him."

"What time is it?" Karen demanded, her dark eyes peering down the hill. Ethan had disappeared into the house, but she kept staring at the front stoop anyway.

"It's too dark. I can't see my watch," Micah replied, holding her watch up close to her face.

Karen flicked on the overhead light.

"It's eleven-twenty," Micah told her.

"I *knew* it!" Karen cried unhappily. "He *was* out with Wendy!"

"Huh? How do you know?" Micah asked.

"The late shift at the Sizzler doesn't end until twelve. He shouldn't be home until twelve-twenty at the earliest."

"Karen!" Micah exclaimed. "You mean you were going to keep us sitting here another *hour*? I don't believe you! I really don't!"

Karen didn't reply. Her gloved hand trembled as she turned the ignition. The Corolla started right up. She jammed it into gear and slammed her foot down on the gas.

"Karen — not so fast! It's slippery!" Micah cried shrilly.

Karen ignored her and lowered her foot on the pedal. The tires spun as the car zigzagged down the hill.

Karen kept her eyes narrowed straight ahead as they sped past Ethan's house. She turned the wheel hard to pull out of a skid, then made a sharp right.

"Karen — slow down! I mean it!"

I don't feel cold anymore, Karen realized. I stopped shivering.

I'm too angry to feel cold. I feel only anger.

Anger and hurt.

"Karen — what is *wrong* with you?" Micah shrieked.

The white light appeared without warning. Twin headlights invading the car, momentarily blinding Karen.

She gasped and raised a gloved hand to shield her eyes.

The headlights grew brighter as the oncoming car roared closer.

"Slow down!"

Karen pumped the brake, but her car went into a skid, sliding toward the center of the street.

Her car slid sideways. Karen frantically spun the wheel, trying to straighten the car out.

Out of control. I'm out of control.

The white light rolled over her like an ocean wave.

"I — can't see!"

The crunch of metal and glass nearly drowned out her scream.

Chapter 3

Karen and Micah were both screaming as the car slid crazily over the street.

Karen's foot pressed the brake down as far as it would go.

Both girls were jolted forward, then sharply back.

The bright headlights vanished from the windshield, casting them in darkness.

The car made a half-spin and stopped at the snowbanked curb.

"Out of control," Karen murmured. "Out of control."

"Are you okay?" Micah asked in a trembling voice.

"Yeah, I guess," Karen managed to reply. "But the crash. I heard — "

"I — I thought — " Micah stammered. She tugged at the sides of her hair with both hands as if holding on for dear life.

Karen stared blankly at the dark windshield. "Did we crash? Is the car wrecked?"

Without waiting for an answer, she pushed open her door and took deep breaths of the cold air. "Oh. Look."

She pointed across the snowy street. Micah leaned over to follow her friend's gaze.

The other car had collided with a telephone pole.

The crash of metal. The shattering glass. It had come from the other car.

We're okay, Karen thought gratefully. We're perfectly okay.

But an inner voice kept her from rejoicing. You *wanted* to crash, the inner voice accused. You were so upset about Ethan, you *wanted* to crash.

Forcing away those thoughts, she wondered if the driver in the other car was okay.

She watched a large man climb out of the car. His boots crunched over the snow as he lumbered toward Karen. "Are you all right?" he called, shouting over the swirling wind.

Karen started to climb out, but the seat belt held her back. "Yeah. We're okay. Your car — "

"Headlight is smashed, that's all." The man stopped a few feet from Karen. He was wearing an enormous coat of some kind of shaggy

fur. It made him look like a bear. Snowflakes
clung to his glasses. "Sure you're okay?"

"Yeah. We didn't hit anything. Just slid,"
Karen replied, shivering. "I'm sorry — "

"Not really your fault," the man said. "I was
going too fast." He motioned for her to close
the door. "You can just leave. I'll get home
okay. It's only a couple of blocks."

Karen watched the man walk back to his
car, the big fur coat ballooning in the wind.
Then she slammed her door shut and slowly
backed the car from the curb.

"You want me to drive?" Micah asked.

Karen could feel Micah's eyes on her, studying her.

"I'm okay," Karen told her. "I'll go slow.
Promise." Karen eased the car through a stop
sign and made a careful left turn.

"This was a fun night," Micah muttered
sarcastically.

"It's all Ethan's fault," Karen replied, surprised at her own bitterness.

"Huh?"

"It's all Ethan's fault," Karen repeated. "He
can't *do* this to me!"

"Do you . . . want to talk about this?" Micah
asked, her expression tight with concern.

"No. I don't think so," Karen replied softly,

her eyes straight ahead on the snow-covered road.

Karen dropped Micah at her house, then hurried home. The snow was turning to frozen sleet as she parked the car in the driveway and let herself in through the kitchen door.

The back of the house was dark. She stopped inside the doorway to pull off her wool cap and boots. Leaving them near the door, she brushed the cold snow from the front of her short, dark hair with one hand.

Then, with a shiver, she made her way to the front stairs. Her mother's bedroom door was closed. Mom must have gone to bed early, Karen decided.

Upstairs, Chris's door was closed, too. She could hear voices from the TV in there. Laughter. Probably *Saturday Night Live*.

Chris loved comedy shows. Sometimes he'd laugh till he had tears in his eyes and couldn't breathe, and Karen would just be sitting there blankly, wondering what he found so funny.

As she passed his bedroom, she suddenly remembered the mannequin stuffed in her trunk. What a dumb joke. She had an impulse to throw open his door and tell him how stupid he was.

Chris was on his winter break from school.

That meant he had a lot of time on his hands. Karen wasn't sure she could take two more weeks of his awful practical jokes.

She hesitated, shivering, her hands and feet nearly numb with cold. Should she go in and get on his case? I think I'd rather just get under the covers and warm up, she decided.

The sound of audience laughter on the TV followed her down the hall. It was warm in her room. Heat poured up from the floor register. Sleet pattered hard against the window. Karen hurried to pull the curtains.

She changed quickly into a long flannel night-shirt, tossing her sweaters and black leggings onto the chair beside her desk.

I'm never going to get warm, she thought, still shivering. Never.

She pulled back the quilt on top of her bed and was about to climb under the covers when the phone rang.

Startled, she jumped at the sound. And glanced at the clock radio beside her bed. Ten after twelve.

Who would call this late? she wondered.

She picked up the receiver midway through the second ring.

"Hello? Micah?"

"No," rasped a deep voice. "This is your worst nightmare calling."

Chapter 4

"Huh?" Karen gripped the receiver tightly in her cold hand. "*Who* is this?"

"Your worst nightmare," the deep voice repeated menacingly.

Karen laughed. "Oh. Hi! How are you?" she cried.

"Okay," the voice replied uncertainly.

"Adam — is your family all moved in? Are you in your new house?" Karen asked, carrying the phone over to the bed and tucking her cold feet under her as she sat on top of the quilt.

"Yeah. We're here," her cousin replied. "I can't believe we're back in Thompson Falls."

"I can't believe it, either," Karen said brightly. "Just like when we were kids. Mom and Dad used to — "

"Have you heard from your dad lately?" Adam interrupted.

"No. He doesn't write," Karen muttered, then quickly changed the subject. "So, how is everything, Adam? Do you like the new house?"

"I don't know," Adam replied. "It makes funny noises. Like groaning and moaning sounds. It's probably haunted. Or it was built on an Indian burial ground or something, and we're all going to be slaughtered in our sleep."

Karen snickered. "You're as cheerful as ever, Adam," she said sarcastically.

"Thanks. How's Chris? How does he like college?"

"You know Chris," Karen replied. "He's fine. He's always fine. He breezes right through everything."

"You still going with that long-haired freak?" Adam demanded.

Karen felt her face grow hot. She had momentarily forgotten how upset and angry she was at Ethan. "You mean Ethan? He isn't a long-haired freak," she said defensively. "Just because he has long hair doesn't mean — "

"Isn't he a little too good-looking for you?" Adam teased.

Karen didn't reply. She wasn't in the mood for her cousin's kidding around. And she especially wasn't in any mood for jokes about Ethan.

She and Adam were nearly the same age. They were both seniors. They had grown up together and had been fairly close, even though they didn't have much in common. They would study together and go to the movies when there was nothing better to do.

Then Adam and his family had moved away from Thompson Falls.

"Adam, it's really late," she said.

"Midnight is late?" Adam laughed scornfully. Then his tone suddenly changed. "Can you do me a favor, Karen?"

"Sure. What?"

"Monday will be my first day at school. I hate coming into a new school in the middle of the year. I mean, I won't know where anything is. I won't even be able to find the boys' room. Do you think if I get there early you could give me a quick tour Monday morning?"

"Sure. No problem," Karen replied. "Meet me a little after eight, okay? Just inside the front door."

"Hey, that's great," Adam told her. He sounded truly grateful.

Adam always was shy, Karen remembered. Moving to a new high school as a senior probably has him really stressed out. "I'll introduce you to some kids, too," Karen promised. "I want you to meet my friend Micah."

"Yeah. Okay. Everyone's probably forgotten me," Adam said with a trace of sadness. "I've been away so many years. Since sixth grade . . ."

He was always kind of a strange guy, Karen remembered. He never had many friends.

"See you Monday morning," she told him, yawning.

"Right. And thanks again, Karen. See you Monday morning." He clicked off.

Karen carried the phone back to her desk, then wearily climbed into bed. Yawning loudly, she forced herself not to think about Ethan.

Ethan and Wendy. Ethan and Wendy.

With their faces floating in her mind, she fell into a dreamless sleep.

She slept late on Sunday morning. It was a little after eleven o'clock when she came down for breakfast, dressed in gray sweats.

Chris was at the kitchen table, his back to Karen, starting his breakfast. He wore a maroon sweatshirt over faded jeans. Mrs. Masters was bent over the dishwasher, loading some dirty plates.

"Morning," Karen muttered. "You slept late, too," she said to her brother.

"Ohhh! My eye!" he cried. "My eye! It's — running!"

He whipped around to face her. He had placed an entire fried egg over his eye.

Karen laughed. She hated to encourage him, but it looked really funny. "You're sick," she told him. She slapped his shoulder really hard, making the egg fall into his lap.

"Chris, grow up," Mrs. Masters said sharply, her hands on her slender hips, a disapproving frown on her face. "I mean, really! How can you be nineteen years old and still be putting fried eggs on your face?"

"Easy," Chris replied, winking at Karen. He lifted the egg off his lap with one hand and plopped it back on the plate. "Want my egg?" he asked Karen. "Only slightly used."

"You want eggs, Karen?" her mother asked, closing the dishwasher.

"Um . . . no. Think I'll just make a Pop-Tart or something," Karen said.

"A Pop-Tart? Since when are you such a health nut?" Chris joked.

"Well, I'm going to run to the mall," Mrs. Masters said, drying her hands. She looked like she could be Karen's older sister. They had the same pale, delicate skin, the same dark brown eyes and brown hair, the same slender, almost frail, figures. "Sunday is my only day to do any shopping."

"Poor Mom." Chris grinned at her. He had yellow egg on his teeth.

"Don't make fun of me," Mrs. Masters scolded, giving the back of his head a playful slap as she passed the table.

Chris rubbed his head. "Hey! Sometimes I get tired of making fun of Karen, you know?" He turned to Karen. "Have you seen my dummy anywhere?"

"Oh, shut up, Chris!" Karen cried angrily. "You scared me to death with that thing last night!"

Chris laughed gleefully. "The body in the trunk!" he cried in his imitation of an eerie monster voice.

"You're not funny. Really. You're just a pain," Karen told him.

She ate her breakfast standing at the sink. Two strawberry-filled Pop-Tarts and a glass of cranberry juice. Then she settled down on the couch in the den, her father's old study, to call Micah.

They talked a little bit about the night before. Then Karen told her about her cousin Adam. "He moved into an old house on Monroe," she told Micah. "Yeah. Just three or four blocks from here. Isn't that weird? He hasn't lived in Thompson Falls since sixth grade. He's starting school on Monday."

"Ooh, he's so weird!" Micah exclaimed. Then she quickly caught herself. "No offense, Karen. I mean, I know Adam is your cousin. But he's definitely weird."

"He's not weird," Karen insisted. "He's just shy. He's terribly shy, Micah."

Micah was silent for a moment. "Does Adam still spend all his time reading those old horror comics and watching old horror movies?" she asked.

"I don't know," Karen told her. "I haven't seen him for ages. I know he used to collect all kinds of horror stuff. He was always really into it. Remember that creepy Halloween costume he made for himself when we were in fifth grade? The one with the green slime pouring out of his nose and mouth?"

"I always thought he was kind of creepy," Micah confessed. "But he's probably changed."

"I want you to be nice to him," Karen instructed, twisting the phone cord around her slender wrist. "He doesn't know anyone. Can you imagine? It's your senior year and you have to leave all your friends behind and move to a new place?"

"I still think he's weird," Micah replied. "But I'll try to be friendly. You know. Give him a break. Maybe he's gotten cute."

Karen suddenly heard a loud ringing sound. "What on earth is that?" she asked.

Micah let out a groan. "It's these hideous chimes my father bought. They go off every hour. They're really gross, but he loves them. Guess it must be twelve o'clock."

She shouted something to her mother. Then she returned her attention to Karen. "Have you heard from Ethan?"

Karen unwrapped the phone cord from her wrist. She had been lying over the arm of the couch. She sat up. "No. Not yet. You know Ethan. He'll probably sleep till noon."

"You're feeling better? I mean, about things?" Micah demanded.

"Yeah. I guess," Karen told her. "Yes. I do. Really."

She wasn't sure how she felt. She had been doing her best to shut Ethan out of her thoughts.

"I was really worried about you last night, Karen," Micah said with concern. "You — you really weren't acting like yourself. The whole idea of spying on Ethan — it was so crazy. And then the way you drove. I — I — "

"I'm feeling a lot better about things," Karen said. "You don't have to worry. I was thinking about it last night, before I fell asleep. You know what I decided, Micah?"

"What?"

"I decided that Ethan cares too much about me. He wouldn't go out with Wendy Talbot. I don't know what I was thinking of. But I know I'm right. I know how much Ethan and I mean to each other. And I know Ethan would never do that to me."

Karen glanced toward the doorway and cried out in surprise.

Ethan took a reluctant step into the room, a troubled expression on his face.

How long has he been listening? Karen wondered. She still held the phone to her ear. "Ethan, what are you doing here?" she asked, unable to hide her surprise.

He lowered his eyes, avoiding her stare. "Uh . . . Karen . . . we've got to talk."

Chapter 5

"Micah, I'll call you later," Karen said, staring hard at Ethan. She hung up the phone and climbed to her feet. "Ethan, hi."

"Hi." He shambled over to the couch, still avoiding her eyes.

He tossed down his jacket, then shoved his hands into the pockets of his baggy, faded jeans. He wore an oversized, pale blue V-necked sweater over a white T-shirt. His long, black hair fell over his shoulders. He had a slender silver ring through one earlobe.

"Chris let me in," he explained uncomfortably. He dropped down onto the big armchair across from the couch.

Karen lowered herself back onto the couch. She sat tensely on the cushion edge. "Where were you last night? I called you," she lied.

"I *told* you," he replied sharply. "I had to work. You know Ernie, that new busboy they hired? He called in sick. So I had to take his shift." He ran a hand back through his long hair. "I didn't get home till after eleven."

"Eleven? I thought the shift ended at twelve," Karen said, trying to sound casual but not quite pulling it off. She fiddled tensely with the sleeves of her gray sweatshirt.

"The restaurant was empty," Ethan replied. "Because of the snow. So they let me go home." He sighed. "Wish I could quit that job. But with my dad laid off . . . you know how it is."

She nodded, studying the troubled expression on his face.

He's so good-looking, she thought. With those soulful, dark eyes. That broad forehead. I wish he'd smile. I love his smile so much.

Why is he here? Karen asked herself. Why does he look so upset? That isn't like him at all. What does he want to talk about?

Do I want to know? Maybe I don't want to hear it.

A heavy feeling of dread rose up from her stomach. She could feel her neck muscles tightening. Whenever she felt stressed out, she immediately got a stiff neck.

"What did you want to talk about?" she asked softly.

Ethan hesitated. He slowly raised his eyes to hers. "Well . . ."

The doorbell rang.

Ethan let out a nervous laugh.

Karen waited to see if Chris was going to answer it. When she didn't hear any footsteps, she hurried to the front door.

She pulled the door open. "Oh. Hi."

"How's it going, Karen?" Jake asked. She stepped aside so he could come in. Jake was Ethan's best friend. He was a tall, wiry, red-haired boy with long, gangly arms. He always reminded Karen of a grasshopper.

Ethan appeared in the front entranceway behind Karen. "Hey, there you are," Jake called to him. Jake had a funny, hoarse voice. A lot of kids called him Frog because of it.

"I've been trying to track you down, man," Jake told Ethan. "Your mom said you might be here."

"Jake, what's your problem?" Ethan asked, a startled expression on his face.

Jake pulled a worn, black leather wallet from his coat pocket. "Here, man. This is yours. You left it at my house last night."

Karen couldn't hold herself back. She turned angrily to Ethan. "Huh? You were at *Jake's* last night?" she demanded shrilly.

Ethan's face turned bright scarlet. "No . . . uh . . ."

Jake held the wallet out to him.

Ethan grabbed it and jammed it into his back jeans pocket. He was still blushing. Karen saw him flash an angry glance at Jake.

What was Ethan doing at Jake's last night? Karen wondered. Why would he break a date with me and make up a lie about having to work just to go over to Jake's?

"I . . . went over to Jake's on my way to the Sizzler," Ethan said finally. His face turned even brighter red.

Jake nodded, unconvincingly.

Ethan is such a terrible liar, Karen thought miserably.

Why is he lying to me? He never lied to me before!

She took a deep breath. She decided she *had* to get the truth out of him.

"Hey, guys!" A voice interrupted from the top of the stairs.

Chris hunched down so they could see him. "How's it going?" Leaning against the banister, he came halfway down the stairs.

Ethan and Jake greeted Chris warmly.

Ethan seems real glad for the interruption, Karen thought unhappily.

"Hey, come upstairs," Chris urged, a devilish grin spreading across his face. "You can all listen in on this call I'm going to make. I'm calling this girl I met."

"Huh? You want us to listen in?" Jake demanded, confused.

"What are you going to do — call her up and make loud breathing sounds?" Karen asked, making a disgusted face. "That's your usual speed."

Chris looked hurt. "Hey, I wouldn't do that." He motioned for them to follow him, then started back up the stairs. "You'll see. It's going to be really funny. Come on. But don't laugh, okay? Don't let her hear you."

Ethan was the first one on the stairs. He hurried up after Chris, taking the stairs two at a time.

He's desperate to get away from me, Karen realized. He's been caught in a lie, and now he's so glad that my stupid brother got him out of trouble.

Jake started up the stairs after Ethan. He turned back to Karen. "You coming?" he called in his hoarse, raspy voice.

"I can't stand my brother's practical jokes," Karen told him, sighing. "But I guess I'll come."

Chris was already dialing the phone when Karen stepped into his room. Leaning over his

desk, his sandy hair falling over his eyes, Chris
grinned at her with the receiver to his ear.

Ethan dropped onto the edge of Chris's un-
made bed. Jake leaned against the closet door.
Karen stayed in the doorway, her eyes on
Ethan.

These phone pranks Chris is always pulling
are so dumb, Karen thought, frowning. Why
does he think they're such a riot?

"Hello, is this Sara Martin?" Chris asked,
disguising his voice, making it deeper. His devilish grin grew wider. "This is David Reston,
your world literature instructor."

Jake let out a high-pitched giggle. Chris
raised a finger to his lips, motioning for him
to be silent.

"I'm glad you're enjoying the class, Sara,"
Chris said, keeping his voice as low as he
could. "But I'm afraid I'm calling with some
bad news."

Chris paused, listening to the girl's surprised reaction.

"Well, I'm afraid I caught you," Chris continued in his deep voice. "I know that you
plagiarized your term report."

Jake slapped his forehead. He was struggling to keep from laughing out loud. Ethan
had a big grin on his face.

I don't think this is funny, Karen thought,

standing stiffly in the doorway, her arms crossed over her chest. It's mean. Chris can be really mean.

"I'm sorry, Sara," Chris continued. "But I know where you copied your report from. You didn't really think you could get away with it, did you?"

That poor girl, Karen thought. She must be so upset.

"There's no point in denying it," Chris was telling the girl. "I know you copied your report from that genius in the class, Chris Masters."

"Oh, brother," Karen said aloud, rolling her eyes.

Chris burst out in laughter. "Yeah. It's me. Hi, Sara. You believed it was Reston — didn't you!"

Everyone in the room was laughing wildly. Everyone except Karen. Sara should hang up on him, she thought. Why is she being such a good sport?

Chris was waving his hand, motioning for Karen and the two boys to leave. Now that the joke was over, he wanted to talk to Sara in private.

Ethan and Jake followed Karen out of the room, still giggling about Chris's joke.

"Your brother is a riot," Jake told Karen.

"Ha-ha," Karen replied sarcastically. "*You*

don't have to live with him." They stopped at the bottom of the stairs. "Know what he did this morning?" Karen continued. "He put a fried egg over his eye."

Ethan and Jake both laughed.

"You think that's *funny*?" Karen demanded. "I think it's pitiful."

The boys laughed again. Then Ethan's expression turned serious. Karen saw the light fade from his brown eyes.

Jake reached for the door, intending to leave.

Karen decided she had no choice. She had to know what was troubling Ethan.

"Ethan, why did you come over?" she asked in a trembling voice. "What did you want to talk to me about?"

Chapter 6

Ethan tossed his long hair behind him with a flick of his head. Jake pulled open the front door. "Come on, Ethan." He tugged Ethan's sleeve. "You promised you'd help me shovel snow."

"Oh. Yeah," Ethan replied. He picked up his jacket. Then he raised his eyes to Karen. "I — I'll call you later, okay?"

"See you," Jake called back to her. He pushed the storm door open, and both boys headed out into the snow.

Karen stood and watched them from behind the glass door as they made their way to Ethan's red Bonneville. Jake reached down with his long, gangly arms and scooped up a handful of snow from beside the driveway. He heaved it at Ethan without bothering to form it into a snowball.

The snow made a white streak on the back of Ethan's jacket. To Karen's surprise, he just kept walking. He didn't bother to retaliate.

Something has really got Ethan upset, Karen knew. He didn't act like himself at all just now.

Did he come over to tell me he wants to go out with Wendy Talbot? Did he come over to break up with me, and then lose his nerve?

The cold seeped in from outside. She slammed the front door shut, but the white glare of the snow stayed in her eyes. She blinked, waiting for her eyes to adjust. Then she hurried to the kitchen to phone Micah and tell her to come over.

Micah obediently arrived about half an hour later. She had her thick, blonde hair pulled back in a loose ponytail. She wore a white sweater over black leggings.

Micah stretched out on her back on the couch in the den, holding one of the square couch pillows between her hands. Karen sat cross-legged on the carpet, her back against an armchair.

"Karen, lighten up," Micah scolded. "You're probably making the whole thing up."

"No, I'm not," Karen insisted glumly. She

rubbed her neck. The muscles had all tightened up.

"You really think he came over here to tell you about him and Wendy?" Micah tossed the pillow up and caught it in both hands.

"He had the strangest look on his face, Micah," Karen said. "You know how laid back Ethan always is. Not today. I could tell he was upset."

Micah tossed the pillow up again. She let it drop through her hands, onto her stomach. "He was probably just tired, Karen. You know. From working so late."

Karen sighed. She stared down at her woolly white socks. When she finally spoke, her voice came out shrill and angry. "If Wendy tries to steal Ethan from me, I'll *kill* her. I really will!"

"Whoa!" Micah sat up abruptly, lowering her feet to the floor. She tossed the pillow at Karen. It bounced off Karen's shoulder. "Stop talking like that!"

"I mean it," Karen insisted. "If Ethan breaks up with me because of her — "

"Listen to yourself," Micah interrupted, her green eyes locked on Karen's. "Listen to how crazy you sound."

"It's *not* crazy!" Karen protested in a shrill voice she didn't recognize.

"How old are you, Karen? You're seventeen, like me, right?"

Karen nodded.

"We're only seventeen," Micah continued emotionally. "We're both going to go out with *lots* of guys."

"No! I want Ethan!" Karen cried. She grabbed the pillow off the floor and heaved it against the wall. "I want Ethan — no one else. I'll kill Wendy. I mean it, Micah. I'll kill Wendy! I really will!"

On Monday morning, Karen woke up early. She pulled herself out of bed and made her way to the window. The sky had finally cleared. A red morning sun was lifting itself above the bare trees.

She dressed quickly, jeans and a sweater over two T-shirts. Then she gave her short, dark hair a quick brush, studying her pale face in the dresser mirror, and hurried downstairs.

Adam will be waiting for his tour of the school, she remembered. Then maybe she could catch Ethan and talk to him before homeroom.

She gulped down a tall glass of orange juice, her usual breakfast. She could hear her mother

bustling about in her bedroom down the back
hall, getting ready for work.

Karen spotted her boots by the kitchen door
where she had left them to dry. Pulling a
kitchen stool over, she sat down, pushed her
left foot into the boot — and started to scream.

Chapter 7

"Chris — I hate you! *I hate you!*" Karen shrieked.

She let the boot fall to the floor and rubbed her wet sock.

Her brother had filled both her boots with snow.

"You creep! You stupid creep!" she cried. Before she realized it, she felt hot tears running down her cheeks.

Chris and their mother both appeared in the kitchen doorway at the same time.

"Karen — what on earth — !" Mrs. Masters cried, her dark eyes narrowed in concern.

Karen's shoulders were heaving up and down. She tried to stop crying, but she couldn't. "It's not funny! Not funny!" she choked out, pointing at the boots.

"Chris — you made your sister cry?" Mrs. Masters demanded sharply, turning to Chris.

"It was just a joke," Chris replied with a shrug. "She's unbalanced, Mom. Look at her. She's really unbalanced."

Karen found Adam waiting in the front hall at school. He greeted her with a smile, his dark eyes coming to life behind his black-framed glasses.

He seemed skinnier than the last time Karen had seen him. He wore his rust-colored hair very short. His chin was dotted with small red zits, she saw. He had a loose-fitting, hooded gray sweatshirt pulled over black denim jeans.

Karen dropped her coat at her locker, then led her cousin on a quick tour, starting with the gym and lunchroom in the basement, and ending up at the wood shop in back on the first floor.

"So? How do you like Franklin High so far?" Karen asked.

Adam shrugged. "So far so good."

He seems as shy and strange as ever, Karen thought. We've known each other our whole lives, but he's as awkward as if he had just met me.

"I just have to remember that the gym and lunchroom are downstairs, and the auditorium is upstairs," he said, scratching his bristly hair.

"I didn't have time to show you the science

lab or the computer room," Karen said, glancing at the clock above their heads. "They're on the third floor."

The hall had filled up with kids eager to stash their coats and get to homeroom. "I'll walk you to your homeroom," Karen offered, shouting over the sound of slamming lockers and loud voices. "Then maybe I'll see you later. I want you to meet my friend Micah."

Adam nodded solemnly.

"Your homeroom is right down here," Karen told him, starting down the hall.

She stopped when she saw Ethan.

He had his backpack slung over the shoulder of his blue-and-gray Franklin High jacket. He was talking to someone, Karen saw, struggling to see him through a crowd of kids.

He was talking to Wendy Talbot.

They were laughing together.

Wendy had her hand on the sleeve of his jacket.

So it's true, Karen thought, holding in a sob. *It's true.*

The crowded scene blurred. The kids shimmered away. The roar of laughing, shouting voices faded to silence.

Karen stood alone. Darkness fell over her like a heavy curtain descending.

I'm alone, she thought.

Everyone has disappeared.

Everyone.

The voices slowly returned, low at first, then as loud as before. The darkness lifted. Someone bumped Karen's shoulder. A girl was shouting, "Michael! Michael! Has anyone seen Michael?"

Karen could see only Ethan. He and Wendy turned away from her, walked side by side in the other direction. They disappeared around a corner.

"Karen — are you okay?" Adam was asking. "Karen?"

She stared down the blurred hallway.

Were those tears in her eyes that were making everything shimmer and bend?

"Karen — are you okay?" Adam demanded.

Staring straight ahead, unable to focus, her knees trembling with the walls, her heart thudding in her chest, the floor twirling beneath her, Karen knew the answer was no.

Micah had been flirting with two boys at the next table. Now she turned back to Karen. "You haven't touched your lunch," she said.

"I know. I can't eat," Karen replied. She crumpled the tinfoil over her sandwich, squeezing it into a tight ball.

"Wait a minute! What is it?" Micah asked. "Is it tuna fish?"

"I don't even know," Karen sighed. She jumped to her feet, the chair nearly falling over behind her.

"Karen — where are you going?" Micah asked, startled. "We still have twenty minutes. You — "

"I'm going to find Wendy," Karen replied in a flat, low voice. The room started to blur again as she said Wendy's name.

I'm not going to cry, Karen told herself, biting down hard on her lower lip. *I'm not going to cry in front of everyone in this crowded lunchroom.*

"Karen, sit down," Micah said sternly. She pointed to Karen's chair. "I mean it. Sit down. You're not going anywhere." Karen didn't budge.

Micah's firm tone turned pleading. "Let's talk, okay? Sit down. Let's talk."

"No, I'm going to find Wendy," Karen said softly, her voice revealing no emotion at all.

"But, Karen — you *can't!*" Micah cried. "She'll just laugh at you. You'll feel like a jerk, Karen. Karen — listen to me!"

Karen didn't reply. She turned and walked toward the lunchroom exit, taking long, determined strides. She could hear Micah calling to her, but she didn't turn around.

A group of cheerleaders were huddled out-side the lunchroom, laughing loudly about something. From down the hall, Karen could hear the *thud* of basketballs from the gym.

Walking quickly, she passed several closed classrooms. Some kids didn't have lunch until the next period.

What would she say to Wendy?

The question jarred through her mind, made her slow her pace.

I'll tell her there's no way she can have Ethan, Karen quickly decided.

I'll just tell her.

She grabbed the metal railing and started up the stairs to the first floor. Two girls head-ing down the stairs called out hello to her as they passed.

Karen didn't reply.

Wendy, where will I find you? she thought.

To her astonishment, Wendy appeared at the top of the stairs.

She was carrying a huge sculpted head in both hands. Some kind of art project.

"Wendy, hi," Karen called breathlessly.

Karen's heart seemed to jump up into her throat. She could feel the blood pulsing at her temples.

She stepped up beside Wendy on the top step.

Wendy's straight red hair glowed in the sunlight from the window against the front wall. She turned her gray-green eyes on Karen. "How's it going?"

How's it going?

How's it going?

The words repeated in Karen's mind like an ugly, threatening chant.

How's it going? You *know* how it's going, Wendy! Karen thought, suddenly bursting with fury.

There was a flurry of motion.

A ripple.

And then thrashing arms.

And suddenly Wendy's sculpted head was flying in the air.

And Wendy was falling, falling backwards, her hands reaching for Karen, grabbing only air.

The papier-mâché head bounced down the hard steps.

Thud. Thud. Thud.

Wendy bounced beside it. Head first.

She let out a low cry each time her head hit a step.

Horrified low cries all the way down to the bottom.

Then she lay sprawled on her back, her arms outstretched, one leg bent under her, her red hair splayed around her unmoving head.

Karen stared down at her from the top step, her hands pressed tightly against her hot cheeks.

Have I killed her? Karen wondered.

Chapter 8

Did I kill her? Karen asked herself.

Did I push her?

Did she fall — or did I push her?

Karen couldn't remember.

The two girls who had been walking down the stairs were huddled over Wendy. Karen didn't move from the top step.

I didn't push her — did I? She fell. I'm sure she fell.

Down below, Wendy groaned, her eyes still shut.

The two girls suddenly raised their eyes accusingly at Karen.

"No, I didn't push her!" Karen shouted. "She fell. I didn't push her!"

And then, Karen was running. Running down the hall.

Her blue Doc Martens slapped the hard floor as she ran.

I didn't push her. I'm pretty sure I didn't push her.

I don't remember. I don't really remember.

Where was Karen running?

She wasn't sure. She just knew she wanted to run forever.

"Karen — could you come downstairs, please?"

Her mother's voice invaded Karen's room. Karen made her way to the bedroom door and opened it a crack. "Mom — I *told* you. I'm not hungry. I can't eat dinner."

Karen had hurried home from school and shut herself up in her room. She glanced at the clock radio. Nearly seven o'clock.

Her eyes moved to her backpack, lying unopened on the floor beside her desk.

What have I been doing all this time? she asked herself. I haven't done any homework. I was lying on the bed, I remember, staring up at the cracks in the ceiling.

Did I fall asleep?

"Karen — come down," her mother insisted. "Or shall I come up?"

Karen pressed her cheek against the bedroom door. "What do you want?" she called down warily.

"To talk," her mother shouted from the bottom of the stairs.

Karen sighed. She didn't want to talk. She *couldn't* talk.

What was she supposed to say to her mom?

"Guess what, Mom? Ethan got interested in another girl, so I pushed her down the stairs today and tried to kill her."

How would that go over?

She hesitated, her face still pressed against the door.

Her mother's footsteps were light and rapid on the stairs. Karen backed away from the door. Mrs. Masters entered, her dark eyes stopping on Karen, her birdlike features set with concern.

"Mom, I'm okay. I'm just not feeling well," Karen said, backing up.

"That was Micah on the phone," Mrs. Masters said, crossing her skinny arms over her chest. She wore a lime-green turtleneck over black corduroy slacks.

"Huh? Micah? She called?" Karen shook her head hard, as if trying to clear it. "Why didn't you tell me?"

"She called to speak to *me*," Mrs. Masters replied softly.

Karen wrinkled her forehead, bewildered.

She slumped down on top of the bed. "How come?"

Mrs. Masters took a few steps toward her, her arms still tightly crossed in front of her. "Micah told me you had a little trouble in school today." Her voice caught on the last word. She coughed and cleared her throat.

"She did?" Karen was confused. What had Micah said? Why had Micah called? What did Micah think she was doing?

"Do you want to tell me about it?" Mrs. Masters asked, her dark eyes piercing so deeply into Karen's that Karen had to look away.

"Not much to tell, really," Karen muttered. *Why don't you leave me alone? Just go away and leave me alone?*

"Micah said you made threats about some girl. A girl named Wendy," her mother said, clearing her throat again.

"Threats? Not really threats," Karen replied, staring down at the worn brown carpet.

"Micah said you made threats in the lunchroom. Then, a few minutes later, this girl fell down the stairs. Micah said the girl had to be taken to the hospital for X rays. That she has a concussion."

"Just a slight concussion," Karen muttered. "She's going to be okay."

"But some kids saw you there. Some kids think you pushed her," Mrs. Masters said softly, her eyes burning into Karen's. "That's what Micah told me."

"No!" Karen cried. "No! That's a lie! That's a stupid lie!" She had meant to stay calm, but her words burst out in a shrill screech.

Her mother's mouth dropped open for a second, revealing her surprise. Her dark eyes flashed, then quickly dimmed. "Karen, you can talk to me," she said with feeling.

She walked up to the bed and placed her hands on Karen's shoulders. "You know you can talk to me, don't you?" she repeated softly. "You can tell me what's troubling you."

"I know, Mom," Karen whispered.

Mrs. Masters leaned down to hug her. Karen sat stiffly, enduring the hug, not moving. Thinking about Micah.

"Well, whenever you're ready to talk, I'm here," Mrs. Masters said softly.

As her mother turned and walked slowly from the room, Karen began to tremble. It took her a while to realize she was trembling in anger. She leapt to her feet, closed her door, and began pacing rapidly back and forth, her hands clasped tightly in front of her.

How could Micah do this to me? she wondered.

How could Micah betray me like this?

I thought she was my friend. My best best friend. Someone I could trust.

So how could she rat on me to my mother?

Why did she call behind my back and tell my mother what happened today?

Karen reached for the phone. She grabbed it with such force, she knocked it onto the floor. The receiver bounced across the carpet. The dial tone buzzed angrily as she stooped to retrieve it.

Her heart pounding, she punched in Micah's number.

Micah picked up after the first ring. "Hello?"

"Micah — why?" Karen cried breathlessly. "I — I don't get it! Why did you do it? Why did you call her?"

"I thought I had to," Micah answered quietly, calmly. "Are you okay, Karen? You sound terrible."

"Why?" Karen repeated. "Why did you tell my mom?"

"For your own good," Micah told her. "I'm worried about you, Karen. Really worried. I thought your mother should know."

Karen could feel her anger rise up, take over. She was losing control —and she didn't care.

"You *betrayed* me!" she shrieked into the receiver.

"Now, wait — " Micah started to protest.

"You're not my friend! You're not! Don't ever talk to me again!" Karen slammed down the receiver.

She realized she was gasping for breath.

"Micah isn't my friend anymore," she said aloud in a choked voice. "Micah isn't my friend."

Ethan is the only one I have left, Karen thought, struggling to slow her racing heart, struggling to make the throbbing in her temples go away.

She rubbed her stiff neck with both hands.

Ethan is the only one left, she told herself.

Ethan squeezed the steering wheel with both hands. He shook his head bitterly. "I can't believe I missed those two foul shots," he sighed.

Karen reached across the seat and placed a comforting hand on the shoulder of his blue-and-gray school jacket. "We won, anyway, Ethan," she said softly. "So it really didn't matter."

"It mattered to *me*," he replied sharply.

They both stared out into the darkness. It was Friday night, and he had driven her home after the game. Parked in her driveway, Ethan left the lights on and the engine running, as if he were eager to leave.

"Want to come in?" Karen asked.

He scowled, still thinking about his missed foul shots.

"No one's home," Karen added. "My brother has a date. My mom is visiting her cousin."

"It was a bad night," Ethan murmured. "I didn't get any rebounds, either. The ball just didn't bounce my way."

"Come on, Ethan. We *won*!" Karen cried impatiently. She tugged his sleeve. "Are you coming in or not?"

His expression changed as he turned to her. He tossed his long hair behind him with a flick of his head. His hands tapped the wheel, pounding a nervous rhythm.

"Karen, there's something I have to tell you," he said in a strange, tight voice. "You're not going to like it. But I have to say it, anyway."

Chapter 9

Karen's breath caught in her throat. She suddenly felt cold all over.

"I — I think we should start seeing other people," Ethan blurted out, speaking quickly, slurring it all into one word. He stared straight ahead, avoiding her eyes.

"Huh?" Karen uttered.

She had been expecting it.

She had been expecting it — but now it came as a total shock.

Was he really breaking up with her?

"We could still go out," Ethan said, turning sheepishly to her. "I mean, we could go out a lot. I still really like you. I mean, we always have so much fun together. We could still go on our bike rides and everything. But — "

"Ethan, what are you *saying*?" Karen cried. She wanted to hold herself together, but her voice came out shrill and choked. And her shoulders were starting to tremble.

He slid his hands tensely over the wheel. "I just think we should see other people, too. There's no reason why we can't — "

"No reason?" Karen shrieked. "No reason?"

"Karen, calm down — okay?" Ethan said impatiently. "Can't we just talk?"

"Talk? What's there to talk about?" Karen cried. "I can see your mind is made up."

"Karen — please — we've always been able to talk to each other. That's one thing I really like about you."

"What's there to talk about?" Karen screamed. A wave of anger swept over her. She felt so angry, so hurt. She had a strong impulse to grab Ethan by the shoulders and shake him, shake him until he understood what he was doing to her.

"We can still go out some Saturday nights," Ethan offered weakly. "And we can still play chess. And — "

"Shut up!" Karen cried, surprised by the violence of her feelings. "Shut up! Just shut up, Ethan!" Tears rolled down her cheeks. "Are you breaking up with me or not?"

"No!" he replied instantly. "I mean . . . well . . ."

"I didn't push her!" Karen shrieked. *"I didn't push her! She fell!"*

Ethan gaped at her in shock.

Tears rolled down Karen's face, blurring her vision, putting Ethan behind a wet curtain, making him seem far, far away.

"Karen, calm down," he pleaded, grabbing her hand. "Calm down. I didn't mean — "

She jerked her hand away. "You can't break up with me! You *can't*!" she insisted, sobbing loudly.

Ethan shook his head helplessly. "I only said — "

"Shut up! I heard what you said!" Karen grabbed the door handle and pushed the door open. A gust of cold air brushed her hot face. Her tears blinded her, making the darkness appear to swim in front of her.

"You can't! You can't!" she screamed.

Without realizing it, she had stumbled out of the car.

Karen, you're totally out of control, a voice said inside her. *Karen, if you don't get control, you'll lose Ethan forever.*

But how can I? she asked herself.

Her legs felt weak. Her knees were quivering. Her chest heaved with each sob.

"I'll call you later," Ethan said, reaching to pull the passenger door shut. "Try to get yourself together, okay? I'll call you when I get home, and we can talk."

Karen turned and ran sobbing around to the back of the house. Ethan's headlights rolled over her as he backed down the drive.

Crazy thoughts jangled through her mind as she fumbled in her bag for her house key. Crazy, frantic thoughts.

I won't let him break up with me.

I'll kill him first. I really will.

Maybe I did push Wendy. I don't care.

What can I say to him? How can I make him change his mind?

Finally, she pulled out the key and managed to push it into the lock with a trembling hand on the third try. She pushed open the kitchen door and closed it quickly behind her.

The kitchen smelled of oranges. The house was dark. She ran to the stairs without turning on any lights. Her heart pounding, her eyes still blurred by tears, she ran up to her room and dropped face down on top of her bed.

"Doesn't Ethan realize how much I care about him?" she said aloud.

She buried her face in the pillow to stifle her sobs. Her crazy thoughts bounced through her mind. She gave in to them, made no attempt to stop them.

After a while, she realized she still had her

coat on. She climbed to her feet, breathing hard. She had stopped crying, but all the tears had given her a sharp headache at both temples.

Rubbing her temples, trying to rub the pain away, she made her way across the room. She clicked on the light — and cried out.

Her old teddy bear had been hung by the neck in the cord to the venetian blind. It drooped limply, its head tilted, its one remaining black eye staring across the room at her.

"Chris — you stupid jerk!" Karen shouted.

How can he be such a creep? she asked herself bitterly.

As she started across the room to rescue the old bear, the phone rang.

It's Ethan! she realized.

What am I going to say? What?

Got to think. Got to think clearly.

How can I make him see how much he means to me?

She picked the phone up in the middle of the second ring. "Hello?" Her voice came out a soft whisper.

"Karen, it's me." Ethan. "I just . . . uh . . . wanted to see how you were doing."

"I — I'm better," she stammered. "You just surprised me, that's all."

"I'm sorry," Ethan replied, but with little feeling. "This is hard, Karen. I hope — "

"I'm sorry I acted like such a jerk," Karen interrupted. She rubbed her throbbing temple with her free hand. "I didn't mean to scream at you like that. You must think — "

"No. Don't worry about it," Ethan said. "I'm just glad you're okay now. I mean, you sound calmer."

"Yeah. I guess," Karen replied. "It's just that — "

"Well, good night," Ethan said. He sounded very eager to hang up. "See you in school."

"Wait, Ethan — uh — I just want to say something to you. I just want to say — "

Karen was interrupted by a loud clicking sound.

"Oh. Hold on, Ethan," she pleaded. "There's a call on the other line. It might be my mother."

More clicking.

"I hate Call Waiting," Karen said. "It always interrupts at the wrong time. Hold on a sec, okay?"

"Okay," Ethan agreed.

More clicks. Then silence.

When Karen returned to Ethan a few seconds later, her voice was trembling and weak.

"Ethan, please — come over! Come over here right away!"

"Karen? What's wrong?" Ethan demanded.

"I'm all alone here, Ethan. Please — hurry! He said he was going to kill me!"

"Huh? Who?"

"The voice on the phone. It was so *horrible,* Ethan. He said he was going to kill me!"

Chapter 10

When Ethan's car pulled up the driveway, Karen ran out to meet him. As he stepped out, she threw herself into his arms, pressing her face against his.

"Ethan — it was so frightening!" she cried.

He kept his arms wrapped around her trembling shoulders.

She pressed her hot face against his. "He — he said such horrible things to me!" she told him.

His arm around Karen's shoulder, Ethan led her into the house. Their shoes crunched over the hard snow. "It was probably a joke," Ethan said softly.

"I — I don't think so," she stammered.

She clicked on the den light, and they sat close together on the couch. She shivered. "The voice — it was just so terrifying!"

She pressed her forehead against his cheek. His long hair tickled her face.

"It was a man?" Ethan asked softly.

"I think so, I couldn't really tell," Karen replied. "The voice was a whisper. Very hoarse. That's what made it so frightening. And then — the things he said. . . ."

"What did he say?" Ethan demanded, tenderly, soothingly stroking her dark hair.

Karen shivered again. "He said such ugly things, Ethan. He said he was going to kill me. He said he knew where I lived, and he was going to kill me. He said that first he would describe how he planned to do it, and then he would do it."

Ethan shook his head. He stroked her hair.

"I — I just kept screaming, 'Who *is* this?' " Karen continued, squeezing Ethan's hand. "I couldn't believe it was happening. I mean, you see stuff like this in movies and on TV. But I couldn't believe it was happening to me."

"It's got to be a joke," Ethan said thoughtfully. "Some kind of sick joke."

"Do you really think so?" Karen asked, holding on to him tightly.

"He'll never call again," Ethan assured her. "You can't let it frighten you. Just forget about it. Really."

Karen shuddered. "That weird, hoarse voice. I'll never forget it. Never! Who would play a joke like that? What kind of sick person?"

"Would you feel better if we called the police?" Ethan asked.

Karen pulled away from him and sat up. "The police? Maybe we should."

Ethan started to his feet. "I'll call them for you."

Karen pulled him back down. "No. Wait. They wouldn't do anything. What would they do? They'd just tell me it was someone's idea of a joke."

"Probably," Ethan replied, frowning.

"I hope it *is* a joke," Karen said, biting her lower lip. "I hope it is. It was so ugly, Ethan. So ugly. I — I'm still shaking."

"It's okay. I'm here now," he said softly. "It's okay, Karen."

He wrapped her in his arms. She leaned into him, raised her face to his, and kissed him until she stopped trembling.

Monday. Dreary Monday, Karen thought unhappily.

As she loaded her backpack to go home after school on Monday, Karen realized it had been a drearier day than most.

She had seen Micah at least a dozen times,

and neither of them had spoken to the other. Karen ate lunch by herself at a table in the corner of the lunchroom. Micah ate with some tenth-grade girls Karen didn't know.

All day Karen had the feeling that kids were staring at her. In the hall just before fifth period, a group of girls suddenly stopped talking as Karen passed.

Were they talking about me? Karen wondered.

Were they talking about me and Wendy?

When the final bell rang, Karen gratefully hurried to her locker, eager to leave. Hoisting her backpack onto the shoulder of her down coat, she stepped out the front exit, into a dark afternoon, the sky cloud-laden and charcoal-colored, nearly as dark as night.

Is it going to snow again? she wondered, lowering her head against the onrushing wind.

She had crossed the street and trudged halfway down the next block when she heard running footsteps behind her.

Was someone coming after her?

Before she could turn her head, two hands grabbed her roughly around the waist.

"It's me, Karen!" a hoarse voice whispered in her ear. "It's me!"

Chapter 11

"Let me go!"

Karen squirmed out of the grasping arms and spun around.

"Adam!" she cried. "Adam — you scared me to death!"

He laughed. He had a silent laugh that sounded more like coughing than laughing. His eyes flashed excitedly behind his glasses.

He shook his head. "You're too easy," he said, giving her arm a playful shove.

"Huh? What do you mean?" Karen demanded, waiting for her heartbeat to return to normal.

"You're too easy to scare. No challenge," Adam said.

What does he mean by that? Karen wondered.

Adam picked up his brown leather briefcase. They started walking, side by side.

Adam had a red-and-white-wool ski cap pulled down over his spiky, rust-colored hair. He wore a khaki-colored coat that was too short for him. His workboots clomped noisily against the sidewalk.

"What's with the briefcase?" Karen demanded. "Isn't that a little dorky? Why can't you carry a backpack like everyone else?"

"I don't like to be like everyone else," he replied. "I like to be different. I *can't* be like everyone else. You know that, Karen."

"But — a briefcase?" Karen cried, staring at it.

"I like it," he replied, swinging it as he walked.

"Well, how's it going?" Karen asked. "Your classes okay? You meet anybody?"

"Yeah. I guess I'm doing okay." They walked in silence for a while. "I thought you were going to introduce me to your friend. Micah."

"I'm not talking to her," Karen told him, feeling her face grow hot.

"Oh. Sorry," he replied.

They stopped at an intersection. A station wagon filled with four enormous barking dogs rumbled past. "Where do you think *they're* going?" Karen wondered.

"Anywhere they want to!" Adam joked. As

they started across the street, his expression turned serious. "You know, some kids think you pushed that girl Wendy down the stairs. I heard them talking today."

"I didn't push her," Karen replied quickly. "She fell."

Karen picked up her pace, keeping her eyes on the black, rolling clouds overhead.

"Wendy is telling everyone you pushed her," Adam reported. "She's trying to get witnesses. You know, kids who saw it. She says she wants to sue you or have you arrested for assault or something."

"That's stupid," Karen replied angrily, making a disgusted face. "There weren't any witnesses."

That remark made Adam stop. He shifted the heavy briefcase to his other hand. "How do you know there weren't any witnesses?"

"There were only two other girls on the stairs," Karen told him. "And they were looking the other way."

Adam studied her face suspiciously. "And Wendy just fell?"

"She slipped, I guess," Karen said uncomfortably.

The wind swirled around them. The sky grew even darker.

A car rolled slowly past. A red car. Karen

turned, thinking it might be Ethan. But it wasn't.

"She's very angry at you," Adam reported, scratching his hair through the wool ski cap. "You'd better stay away from her," he warned.

"No problem," Karen replied dryly. They started walking again, lowering their heads against the strong wind. "Maybe Wendy made the phone call," she added in a low, thoughtful voice.

"What? What phone call?" Adam asked.

She told him about the hoarse, whispering voice that threatened to kill her.

"Weird," Adam muttered, shaking his head. "Did you tell your mother?"

"Not yet," Karen replied. "Ethan said it was a joke. A one-time thing. And if it was just a one-time thing, I didn't want to tell my mom and get her all worried."

"Yeah. Right," Adam said thoughtfully, his eyes narrowed behind the black-rimmed glasses. "It's a one-time thing, Karen. I'm sure it's a one-time thing."

"So are we going to the new dance club Saturday night?" Karen asked. She sat on the edge of her desk chair, cradling the phone between her chin and shoulder as she brushed clear polish onto her nails.

It was a little after seven-thirty Monday evening. A frozen rain pattered against the bedroom window behind her.

On the other end of the phone line, Ethan hesitated. "I don't know. I may have to work."

Is he lying to me? Karen wondered.

Why does he sound as if he's lying? Am I just being paranoid?

"You worked *last* Saturday — remember?" she said crossly.

"I know," Ethan sighed. "I have to talk to Tony. At the Sizzler. If I can trade shifts with Tony, then you and I can go out Saturday."

He's lying, Karen decided.

He's definitely lying. He plans to go out with Wendy on Saturday night, and he's making up a story so he doesn't have to tell me the truth.

"I really want to see you," she cooed. "Last Saturday was so terrible."

"I know. I hope I can trade shifts," Ethan replied. "But if Tony — "

He was interrupted by loud clicks.

"Oh. Wait. That's the Call Waiting," Karen said, annoyed. "Hold on. It might be my mom. She's working late."

She clicked off.

A few seconds later, she returned to him. Once again, her voice was shrill and frightened. "Oh, Ethan — it was him again!"

Ethan groaned. "Oh, no."

"He — he said he was going to cut my throat!" Karen cried.

"Try to calm down," Ethan advised. "Did you recognize the voice? Could you tell who it was?"

"No," Karen told him. "He said he was closer than I knew. He said he could get into my house any time he wanted. Then he said he was going to cut my throat!"

She let out a frightened sob. "It was so horrible, Ethan! So horrible!"

"I'll be right over," Ethan said.

"Please — hurry!" she cried. "He said he could get into my house — any time he wanted!"

She hung up the phone.

Staring down at her wet nails, she saw a dark shadow move in the mirror.

She opened her mouth to scream, but no sound came out.

And then the dark figure lurched across the room and grabbed her.

Chapter 12

"Gotcha!" a voice shouted.

Karen gasped in terror and spun around.

"Chris!"

He tossed back his head and opened his mouth in a fiendish, horror-movie laugh. "Made you jump!" he cried triumphantly.

"Chris — you jerk!" Karen screeched. "You're not funny! You're not funny! Leave me alone!"

Karen leaned over the desk and buried her face in her hands. Her trembling shoulders revealed to Chris that she was crying.

"Hey — what's wrong?" he demanded. She felt his hand on her back. "What's your problem, Karen?"

She kept her face buried in her hands, wishing he would just go away.

"I'm sorry," Chris apologized. "It was just

a joke. I'm sorry. What's wrong, Karen? Why are you so upset?"

Ethan arrived a few minutes later, his long hair disheveled, his features set in a worried frown.

He tossed his jacket over the banister and followed Karen into the den. He was dressed all in black, a black sweater over black denim jeans. "Whose funeral is this?" Karen asked dryly.

"Don't be so morbid," Ethan replied.

Chris was already in the den, staring out the window. He turned when Ethan entered and greeted him with a grunt.

Ethan sat close beside Karen on the couch in the den. He kept clasping and unclasping his hands, cracking his knuckles.

Chris paced back and forth across the small room, shaking his head, glancing at his sister. "You should put cold water on your eyes," he advised her. "They're all red and bloodshot."

"I'm okay," Karen replied quietly, raising her eyes to Ethan.

Chris stopped in the middle of the room and leaned his weight on the back of the armchair. "You look worse than Karen does," he told Ethan. "You're as pale as a ghost."

Wind rattled the den window behind her. Karen felt cold air on the back of her neck. She tapped her fingers nervously on the soft arm of the couch.

"I'm just worried about Karen," Ethan told Chris, leaning forward tensely. "She told you about the calls, right?"

Chris nodded.

"What if this creep is serious?" Ethan demanded.

"Maybe we *should* call the police," Karen said thoughtfully.

Chris shook his head. "They'll say it's a dumb joke, which it is."

"How do you know for sure?" Ethan demanded.

"It's either a kid from school," Chris replied, "or it's some nut who just stays home and makes threatening calls. We studied these guys in a psychology unit last semester. I read all about them."

Karen let out an angry groan. "Chris — this is really happening," she said sharply. "It's not a case history in one of your psych textbooks."

She tugged at the sides of her short, brown hair. "I can't believe this is happening to me."

Another strong blast of wind outside made the window rattle again. Karen snuggled against the sleeve of Ethan's sweater.

"These guys never leave their houses," Chris continued, still leaning against the back of the chair. "Most of them are afraid to go out and face the real world. So they stay inside and make sick phone calls."

"But why me?" Karen cried shrilly. "Why did he choose me?"

"Are you sure it's a he?" Ethan asked, raising his arm and draping it around her shoulders.

"Yeah. Could you recognize the voice?" Chris demanded.

Karen shook her head. "I couldn't. Whoever it is just whispers. A very hoarse whisper. Like someone with really bad laryngitis."

"Well, next time, just tell him to drop dead, and then hang up," Chris advised. "Look at you." He shook his head disapprovingly, his sandy-colored hair falling over his forehead. "You're a total wreck."

"Chris is right," Ethan told her. "You can't let yourself get all upset. Just tell the creep to drop dead."

Karen started to reply, but the phone rang.

Chapter 13

Karen grabbed the couch arm. She raised her eyes to Ethan.

Ethan jumped to his feet, his hands balled into tight fists at his sides.

Chris hesitated, staring at the phone on the desk against the window. It rang twice. Then he moved quickly across the room and picked up the receiver in the middle of the third ring.

"Hello?" he shouted. "Who is this?"

Her eyes on her brother, Karen crossed her arms over her chest as if shielding herself. Ethan stood tensely beside the couch, also staring at Chris.

"Oh. Hi," Chris said. "How's it going?" His solemn expression gave way to a smile. "Hold on." He pointed the receiver toward Ethan. "It's for you. It's Jake."

"Huh? Jake?" Ethan's expression revealed relief and surprise. He glanced back at Karen as he made his way to the phone. "Now you've got *me* freaked!"

Ethan turned his back to Karen and began talking in low tones to Jake.

"You going to be okay?" Chris asked with genuine concern.

"Yeah. I'm feeling a lot better," Karen replied, forcing a smile. "Really. I'm sure you're right about the calls. Being harmless, I mean."

Chris glanced at the desk clock. "Mom is really putting in long hours," he muttered. "Well, okay. I'm meeting some friends. Tell Mom I said hi. Tell her I'll be in pretty late."

He gave her a little wave, glanced at Ethan, who still had his back turned, and disappeared from the room.

Karen rubbed her sleeves with both hands. The cold air was seeping right through her sweater. This den has always been the coldest room in the house, she thought.

She watched Ethan leaning over the desk. The light caught the silver ring in his ear and made it glow. She loved the way his hair flowed over his collar. She wanted to touch it, tug at it, pull it through her fingers.

When Ethan finally hung up the phone, she motioned for him to come sit beside her on the couch.

"I can't," he said, lingering by the desk.

"I've got to go help Jake. He can't get the math. He begged me to come over and do it with him."

"Oh." Karen sighed. She couldn't conceal her disappointment.

Ethan started to the door, then stopped. "You'll be okay, won't you?"

"Yeah. I guess," she replied uncertainly, her arms still wrapped around herself. She lowered them and climbed to her feet.

"You won't get any more weird calls tonight," Ethan told her.

She followed him to the front door. "Why don't you stay and help me with *my* math?" she asked teasingly, giving him her most inviting smile.

He smiled back at her. "Because you don't need any help with your math," he replied. "Jake is hopeless. Jake can't do long division."

He picked up his jacket and pulled it on. Then he kissed her, a short peck.

She reached to put her arms around his shoulders. But he turned and hurried out the door. "Later!" he called back to her as the storm door slammed behind him.

What's your hurry, Ethan? Karen thought sadly, staring out into the darkness.

Why are you in such a big rush to get away?

* * *

She didn't have a chance to talk to Ethan again until Thursday after school. He always seemed to be hurrying somewhere — to basketball practice, to work, or to Jake's.

Her heavy backpack slung over one shoulder of her down coat, Karen was on her way out of the building when she saw Ethan at his locker. "Hey — hi!" She called to him and went running over.

"What's up?" He greeted her with a quick smile. "You look great. What did you do to your hair?"

"Washed it!" Karen laughed. "You're not going to basketball practice?"

"Coach canceled it for today," Ethan replied. "He had to go somewhere."

"Good!" Karen declared. "Then you can come home with me, and we can study together." She brought her face close to his and whispered teasingly in his ear, "Or *not* study."

"Can't," he replied flatly. "They put me on the early shift tonight. At the Sizzler. I'm already late." He pulled his jacket out of the locker. A stack of books toppled out onto the floor. He bent down to retrieve them.

"You've been working a lot," Karen remarked, biting her lower lip.

"Yeah. We really need the money," Ethan replied, shoving books back onto the locker floor. "Oh. I'm sorry. I've got bad news. I meant to call you last night. I couldn't switch shifts with Tony."

She stared down at him. "You mean — ?"

"I can't take you to the dance club Saturday night," he said, avoiding her eyes. "I've got to work."

"Ethan!" Karen cried emotionally. "I'm really disappointed."

"Me, too," he replied softly. He still refused to look her in the eye.

Through gritted teeth, Karen asked Ethan to call her after work. He said he'd try.

Feeling really annoyed, she offered a curt good-bye and made her way toward the front exit, taking long, angry strides. She passed a group of laughing kids, heading to play rehearsal in the auditorium.

The building was quickly emptying out. Two blue-uniformed cleaning people were dragging mops and buckets from a small supply closet.

Karen turned another corner, headed down the hall, and nearly ran into Micah. Micah had her back to Karen. She was tugging at her tangles of blonde hair with one hand as she talked quietly to someone, standing very close.

Jake!

Karen was astonished to see Micah talking so cozily to Jake.

Sure, Micah would flirt with almost any boy. But she never could stand Jake, Karen thought, hesitating in the middle of the hall. So how come they're suddenly such good pals? Weird!

She watched them talking. Jake wore a black vest over a white T-shirt. Micah gave the vest a friendly pat.

Weird. Very weird, Karen thought.

Jake spotted Karen first. "Hi, Karen!" he called to her in his hoarse voice.

Micah spun around. "Karen!" Her green eyes opened wide with surprise.

Karen turned and started to jog in the other direction.

"Karen — come back!" she heard Micah call after her. "Karen — this is stupid! We've got to talk!"

Karen slowed her pace for a moment. Maybe I *should* stop and talk with her, she thought.

But she realized she'd be too embarrassed now. She'd already started to run away.

She turned the corner, ran past the two cleaners who had already started to mop the floor, past the auditorium where loud piano music came drifting out, around another corner

— where she nearly collided with Wendy.

"Oh!" Karen cried out, startled.

She gazed past Wendy down the long corridor. Empty. No one else in sight.

Wendy's eyes narrowed angrily. Something gleamed in Wendy's hand. She raised it toward Karen.

"Wendy — no!" Karen shrieked. "Put down the gun!"

Chapter 14

Karen's breath caught in her throat as Wendy lifted the gun higher.

The gun shimmered in front of Wendy's olive-green T-shirt. Wendy's straight, red hair caught the light from the ceiling.

"Wendy, please — !" Karen pleaded.

A strange smile formed on Wendy's face. "Karen, what's your problem?" she asked, her gray-green eyes narrowing as she studied Karen's alarmed face. "You *know* I'm the prop master for *Guys and Dolls*." She gestured toward the auditorium with the pistol. "They need this for the rehearsal."

Karen could feel her face grow hot. She knew she was blushing. She shifted her backpack to her other shoulder. "I thought — "

"Have you lost it totally?" Wendy asked scornfully, tossing her straight red hair back with a flick of her head. She laughed. "Did you think it was a real pistol? Did you really think I was going to shoot you?"

"No. Of course not," Karen lied. "I just thought — "

"Bang-bang," Wendy said, rolling her eyes. She pointed the prop gun at Karen's stomach.

Karen stared at her awkwardly, waiting for her normal breathing to return, waiting for her heart to stop pounding.

"I've got to go. I'm late. The rehearsal already started," Wendy said, starting past Karen.

"You know, I *didn't* push you!" Karen blurted out. She felt her face grow even hotter.

"I know," Wendy replied quickly, her face revealing no emotion at all.

"Huh?" Her words caught Karen by surprise.

"I know," Wendy repeated. "I was off balance. That stupid papier-mâché head started to slip out of my hands. I grabbed for it and fell."

"Oh," Karen replied, feeling foolish. "I — well — some kids were saying things. They said you thought I pushed you." She lowered her eyes from Wendy's stare.

"No. You didn't push me," Wendy said quietly. "But you didn't stay to help me, either."

Her expression turned hard. Her eyes burned into Karen's. "You didn't stay to see if I was okay. You didn't bother to come down the stairs. I saw you, just staring down at me from the top step."

"I — I know," Karen stammered, feeling her neck muscles tighten. "I was upset. I was scared. So . . . I ran. I just panicked, I guess."

Wendy sniffed, but didn't reply. "I've got to go." She gestured again with the silvery pistol.

"I know about you and Ethan," Karen said, letting the words spill out in a rush.

"What? What are you talking about?" Wendy asked scornfully.

"You can stop pretending," Karen said, staring down the long, empty hall. A jangle of piano music floated into the corridor as someone opened the auditorium door. Someone was pounding the keyboard crazily.

"Karen, I really don't know what you're talking about," Wendy said in a low, deliberate voice.

"It doesn't matter," Karen told her heatedly. "It doesn't matter because Ethan is back with me now. That's the truth. He isn't breaking up with me, Wendy. He isn't interested in you anymore."

Wendy rolled her gray-green eyes again.

"Wow, Karen — get a reality check!" she exclaimed.

"Wendy, I'm serious — " Karen insisted.

"I've got to go," Wendy said sharply. She brushed past Karen and disappeared around the corner.

Karen stood staring down the empty hallway, Wendy's footsteps fading behind her.

I confronted her, Karen thought. I said everything I wanted to say to her.

So why don't I feel better about things?

Why do I feel so much worse?

She slumped into the blue Corolla and drove aimlessly around Thompson Falls for a while. Sometimes cruising around town helped to calm her.

But not today.

As Karen made her way through the wintergray streets, she kept seeing Wendy's sneering face.

I hate that smug look of hers, Karen thought. So smug and superior. Like she knows a secret that I don't.

A secret . . . a secret . . .

Karen stopped for a red light. She tapped the wheel tensely with both hands, picturing Wendy, her red hair, her laughing green eyes . . . the stupid prop pistol in her hand.

She deliberately scared me, Karen decided. I know she did.

She was waiting for me. She heard me coming. She raised the pistol to give me a scare.

"Whoa!" Karen murmured out loud, pushing her foot down on the gas as the light changed. She roared into the intersection. "Whoa, Karen. Let's not become a *total* paranoid! Let's not lose it completely here, girl!"

She drove past the school for the second time. A few kids had been let out of the *Guys and Dolls* rehearsal and were huddled on the front walk. A guy Karen knew was trying to balance on the metal railing beside the walk, flailing his arms in the air, finally leaping to the ground in defeat.

The back of Karen's neck ached. She rubbed it with one hand. The muscles were tight and hard.

She turned onto Jackson and kept driving. Houses and yards rolled by in a gray blur. Karen rolled through a stop sign without noticing.

She couldn't shake Wendy from her thoughts.

Why did she laugh at me and tell me to get a reality check? Is it because she and Ethan really are seeing each other?

No, Karen told herself. No, no, no.

The Sizzler suddenly came into view on the right.

Ethan is working in there, she realized.

On an impulse, Karen turned the wheel sharply, into the parking lot.

I've got to talk to Ethan, she decided. Ethan will cheer me up.

He didn't like for her to visit while he was working. The restaurant manager was really strict. She was always on Ethan's case for one thing or another.

I'll only stay for a few minutes, Karen decided, sliding the car into a parking space in front of the entrance.

There were only two other cars in the lot. She climbed out and stretched, straining to see into the restaurant through the glass doors. The aroma of charcoaled steak floated out to greet her.

Taking a deep breath, Karen pulled open the door and stepped inside. Bright white lights beamed down on the vast salad bar in the center of the room.

At first, she didn't see anyone in the restaurant at all. Then she spotted an elderly couple sitting across from each other in a blue vinyl booth against the far wall.

A waitress walked past the salad bar, a tray of water glasses tinkling in her hands. Two white-uniformed food servers stood behind the long counter to Karen's right.

It's so quiet in here, Karen thought, her eyes searching for Ethan. I guess it gets busier in a few hours at dinnertime.

I'll only stay a minute, she told herself.

Just seeing Ethan will cheer me up.

She took a few steps toward the rows of booths to get a better view.

No Ethan.

He must be in the kitchen, she decided.

"Would you like a table?" a young man with spiky black hair stepped up to her with an eager smile. "One for dinner?"

"No," Karen said, shaking her head. "I'm looking for someone. Ethan Parker. He works here."

"Ethan Parker?" the young man scratched his spiky hair and looked around. "Oh, wait. I just started. Here's the manager." He turned and called to a middle-aged woman at the end of the food counter. "Does an Ethan Parker work here?" he called.

The woman came walking over, her eyes trained on Karen. "Ethan? Are you looking for Ethan?" she asked.

Karen nodded. "I just need to see him for a minute."

"Well, Ethan doesn't work here anymore," the woman told her.

"Huh?" Karen gaped at her in surprise.

"Ethan quit two weeks ago," the woman said.

Chapter 15

Karen nervously pulled the hairbrush through her hair. She tossed the brush down. It bounced off the dresser top and onto the floor, but she made no attempt to pick it up.

I *hate* the way I look, she thought, frowning at herself in the oval dresser mirror.

Why do I keep my hair so short and ugly? Why don't I color it so it isn't so lifeless and dull? Why don't I wear a little makeup so I'm not always so ghastly pale?

Why can't I have big green eyes like Wendy?

Wendy. Wendy. Wendy.

Ethan and Wendy.

The names repeated in Karen's mind like an endless, mind-numbing chant.

Ethan quit his job at the restaurant so he could spend time with Wendy. He lied to me. He lied to me again and again.

What am I going to do?

She took a deep breath and held it.

Calm down, Karen, she instructed herself. Calm. Calm . . .

Letting the air out in a whoosh, she strode quickly to her desk. She picked up the phone receiver and punched in Ethan's number.

His mother picked up on the second ring.

"It's me. Karen. Can I speak to Ethan?"

"We're just finishing dinner, Karen," Mrs. Parker replied. "Can he call you later?"

"N-no," Karen stammered. "I'll only take a minute."

A few seconds later, Ethan was on the other end.

"Hi," Karen said uncertainly. Now that she had him on the phone, she began to lose her nerve. She was no longer sure she wanted to confront him.

"What's up?" Ethan asked brightly.

Something about the cheeriness of his voice strengthened her resolve. Ethan, you lied to me, she thought. And now you sound so cheerful because you think you're getting away with it.

"Ethan, I went to the Sizzler after school." The words tumbled out in a hard, tight voice. "I wanted to talk to you. But they told me you don't work there anymore."

Silence.

A long silence on Ethan's end.

Then, finally, he found his voice. "Yeah. I know. I quit. I've been meaning to tell you."

"Well, why didn't you?" Karen demanded shrilly.

"I . . . thought you'd be upset. I mean, I didn't want you to think I was a quitter."

Pretty lame, Karen thought, twisting the phone cord tightly around her wrist. *Even I could come up with a better excuse than that.*

"The job — it was interfering with my schoolwork. I was falling behind," Ethan continued. The more he talked, the less convincing he sounded. "So my parents said I should quit."

"Two weeks ago," Karen said through clenched teeth.

"Yeah. I've been meaning to tell you. Really," he insisted. "I mean, that's why I haven't been able to go out with you as often. Because I haven't had any money."

Liar! Liar! Karen thought bitterly.

"Well, I have a little money," she told him.

"Yeah, but — "

"If you're not working anymore, that means we can go out Saturday night, right? We can go to the dance club?"

Silence.

"Well, I'm not sure — " he started.

But they were interrupted by loud clicks.

"Oh, that's my Call Waiting!" Karen moaned. "Hold on, Ethan. Don't go away." Her voice trembled. "I hope it isn't that creep again. He really scares me so much!"

Another click. Nearly a minute of silence.

Then Karen returned to Ethan. "Ethan — can you come over?" she pleaded breathlessly. "It — it was him."

"Karen — try not to get upset," Ethan urged.

"I can't help it!" she cried. "He said the most ugly things, Ethan. Please — hurry over! He said he can see me! He said he can see me whenever he wants!"

"Karen, please. Take a deep breath," Ethan instructed.

"He said he was coming to cut my throat!" Karen cried frantically. "He said he's coming soon!"

"Karen — ?"

"Oh, please, Ethan — hurry over! You've got to help me! We've got to figure out who is doing this! We've got to stop him. It isn't a joke, Ethan. He — he really means it. I can tell!"

Karen uttered a tiny cry. "Oh — Ethan! The doorbell! I just heard the doorbell!"

Chapter 16

Karen hurried downstairs to answer the door. The front room was dark. She was the only one home. Her mother was working late. Chris was out with friends.

She stopped at the front door, breathing hard, and brought her face close to the wooden door. "Who is it?"

Silence. And then a deep, fiendish laugh.

Karen pulled the door open. "Adam? What are *you* doing here?"

"I've come to drink your blood!" Adam declared in a thick Bela Lugosi-vampire accent. His reddish eyebrows flew up over his black-rimmed eyeglasses, and he raised both hands as if to attack Karen.

"Adam, I'm a little stressed out right now," Karen sighed. "I'm really in no mood for kidding around."

"Who's kidding?" Adam insisted. He

stepped past her into the living room. He was wearing the too-short, khaki-colored jacket he always wore, zipped up to the neck. He had both hands buried in the pockets. "Is your mom home?" He peered through the dark room toward the den.

Karen shook her head. "No. Mom is working late, as always. And Chris is out somewhere, probably getting into trouble."

"How come you're so stressed out?" Adam demanded, his eyes studying her through his glasses.

Karen shrugged. "I just am." She really didn't feel like discussing the phone calls with Adam. She had told him about the first one. But she didn't feel like getting into it with him now.

Besides, what could *he* do to help?

"Adam, did you come over just to chitchat?" she asked impatiently.

He shook his head. "No. I wondered if I could borrow your history notes. The French Revolution notes from yesterday?"

"Yeah, I guess. I have them upstairs," Karen told him. "But I'll need them back for this weekend."

"I'll copy them over and bring them back tomorrow," Adam replied. "Promise."

She started up the stairs to her room to get

the notes. He followed close behind.

"I love the French Revolution," he said, a strange grin forming on his pale face. "All those beheadings."

"Yuck," Karen muttered, pulling her history notebook from her backpack.

"Slice!" Adam made a chopping motion with one hand.

"Stop!" Karen pleaded.

"Don't you wonder about all those heads?" he asked, still grinning. "I mean, what did they do with the heads after they cut them off? Just toss them aside? Or did they bury the head with the body? Do you think they sewed the head back on the person and then buried him? Or did they bury the head by itself? You know. In a square hat box or something."

"Adam, you really are making me sick," Karen murmured, rolling her eyes. She handed him the notebook.

"Can't you just imagine all the blood and guts pouring out of the neck, and the head rolling around on the guillotine platform? The history text really does a very poor job of describing it."

"Thank goodness!" Karen declared. "You really are weird — you know?"

"I'm just really into history," he replied.

She gave him a playful shove toward the door. "Go home, Adam."

His expression suddenly turned serious. "Have you gotten any more scary phone calls, Karen? Is that why you're so stressed out?"

"Yeah. I got another one," she confessed. "Just a few minutes before you showed up."

"Really?"

"It was very scary," Karen told him. "Very threatening."

She tried to read the expression on Adam's face. Was that a half-smile he was struggling to hide?

What *was* that frightening expression?

He started to the door. "I guess I was wrong about it being a one-time thing," he said softly. "Maybe you'd better take those calls seriously."

A few minutes after Adam left, the front doorbell rang again. Karen had returned to her room to study. She slammed the textbook shut at the sound of the bell and jumped to her feet.

"It must be Ethan!" she declared out loud.

She hurtled down the stairs two at a time and pulled the door open. "Ethan?"

No.

Peering out into the darkness, Karen gasped in shock.

Chapter 17

"Micah!" Karen cried in astonishment.

"I've got to talk to you," Micah called through the storm door. Her eyes burned into Karen's through the glass.

"No. We don't have anything to talk about," Karen said coldly.

"Karen, let me in," Micah called impatiently. She grabbed the storm door handle and pulled the door open.

"Micah, I'm busy," Karen insisted. But she stepped back so that Micah could enter.

Micah had her thick, blonde hair pulled back and tied loosely with a blue ribbon. She wore a pale blue down vest over a bulky yellow sweater, and faded denim jeans with a hole in one knee.

Karen led her into the living room and stood in front of the couch. She crossed her arms in front of her and didn't sit down.

Micah made a disgusted face. She stood awkwardly in the middle of the room. "I thought you and I were friends," she murmured.

"I thought so, too," Karen replied coldly. "But I guess not."

What is she doing here? Karen asked herself. She isn't my friend any longer. She's a traitor. A *traitor*!

"I'm really worried about you," Micah said, ignoring Karen's sneer.

"Worry about yourself," Karen snapped.

"No. Really," Micah continued. She stepped closer, her green eyes studying Karen. "Listen to me, Karen. You and I are friends, and — "

"We *were* friends," Karen interrupted, sadness creeping into her voice. She struggled to keep herself together.

Micah turned away. "I'm sorry you feel that way," she murmured.

"That's the way I feel," Karen insisted angrily.

Micah cleared her throat. Her charm bracelet jangled as she lowered her hands to her sides, balling them into tight, tense fists. "Ethan isn't worth it," she said, her voice barely above a whisper.

"Huh?" Karen wasn't sure she had heard correctly.

"I came here to tell you that Ethan isn't worth it," Micah repeated emotionally. "He really isn't."

"You know for sure about him and Wendy?" Karen asked.

Micah started to say something, but changed her mind.

"Come on, Micah — tell me what you know!" Karen demanded shrilly. "Tell me!"

Micah shook her head sadly. "He isn't worth it, Karen."

"Tell me!" Karen cried.

"I — I can't talk to you," Micah said, starting toward the door. "I can see that. I can't talk to you now." She made her way quickly to the front door, taking long strides.

Karen chased after her. "Tell me what you know!" she insisted. "Isn't that why you came here, Micah? To make sure I know the truth about Ethan and Wendy?"

Micah turned with her hand on the storm door handle. "I'm sorry," she said softly. "Really sorry." Micah hurried out the door.

Breathing hard, Karen leaned her back against the solid door and waited for her heart to stop pounding.

I really lost it, she realized. I totally lost it. Micah must think I'm crazy.

Why did Micah come? What did she want?

Karen's brain was spinning too wildly to figure it out.

Did Micah come to warn her? To tell her some news about Ethan and Wendy?

To help her?

No way to tell.

Maybe if Karen hadn't started screaming at her, Micah might have explained why she had come.

I've got to get control, Karen told herself. I'm just so stressed out. . . .

Karen made her way to the kitchen and put the kettle on. Some hot chocolate will help calm me down, she thought.

As she reached into the cabinet for a mug, the phone rang. She hurried over to the wallphone and picked it up. "Hello?"

"Hi, Karen. It's me."

Ethan.

"Oh, hi. I thought you'd be here by now," she told him.

"I can't come," Ethan said hesitantly. "I'm sorry, Karen. But my parents need the car. And they need me to stay here with my little cousin."

"Oh," Karen replied, unable to hide her disappointment. "Well — "

"Will you be okay? Do you think you should call the police?" Ethan asked.

"I don't know," she told him. "I don't know what to do."

"When is your mom getting home?"

"Soon," she replied, glancing over the sink at the kitchen clock. "Any minute, I guess."

"Good," Ethan said, sounding relieved. "Then you'll be okay?"

"I guess," she replied doubtfully.

"Oh — Saturday night. We can go to the dance club," Ethan told her. "If you still want to."

"Great!" she exclaimed, brightening. "That's excellent, Ethan!"

He's going out Saturday night with *me*! she thought happily. Me — not Wendy!

They chatted for a while longer. Ethan urged her to call the police about the creepy calls. She replied that she might.

When the kettle started to whistle, she said good night and hung up.

She was crossing the kitchen to the stove when she saw the broom closet door move.

It made a soft creaking sound as it slid open a fraction of an inch.

Karen gasped. She locked her eyes on the closet door.

Another soft creak.

The door edged open another fraction of an inch.

Karen raised her hands to her cheeks. "Who — who's there?" she managed to choke out.

The door creaked again, louder this time.

It swung open all the way.

And as Karen gaped in horror, Chris's body tumbled heavily to the floor.

Chapter 18

Karen cried out as Chris's body landed hard on its side. It bounced once, then lay still, one arm folded underneath it, one leg bent at an impossible angle.

"Chris — Chris — ?"

Had he been murdered and stuffed into the broom closet?

She took a reluctant step toward the unmoving body.

Was her brother lying dead on the floor in front of her?

Or was this another dumb practical joke?

Yes. Another dumb joke, she thought desperately. Please, please — make it another dumb joke.

Chris grinned at her. "I can't keep a straight face," he said. "You look so totally freaked, I can't keep a straight face."

"You didn't fool me," she lied. She breathed

a long sigh. "I knew you were faking."

"Liar. You're a liar, Karen. You fell for it. You should have seen your face. It was great!" Laughing in triumph, Chris pulled himself to his feet.

"When did you get home?" Karen demanded, ignoring his gloating grin.

"A few minutes ago," he told her. "I heard you heading for the kitchen. So I ducked into the closet. I couldn't resist."

"Your jokes are going to kill me, Chris," Karen said, shaking her head unhappily. "They really are."

Saturday night, Karen was drying her hair when she heard the doorbell ring downstairs. "Chris — could you answer it?" she called to her brother in the next room. "It's Ethan. Tell him I'm still getting dressed."

She listened for Chris's footsteps on the stairs, then returned to her hair.

Chris pulled open the door and greeted Ethan. "How's it going?"

Ethan stepped inside. He shook himself as if trying to shake off the cold. "It's brutal out there, man," he muttered to Chris.

The wind slammed the storm door against the side of the house. Ethan grabbed it and struggled to pull it shut.

"What a winter," Chris said, closing the front door behind Ethan. "Is that wind ever going to stop? It's almost like a hurricane out there."

"Tell me about it," Ethan muttered. He glanced up the stairs. "Is Karen ready?"

Chris shook his head. "I heard her hair dryer going."

"Is she okay?" Ethan asked tensely. "She didn't get any more scary phone calls, did she?"

"No. I don't think so," Chris replied. "I think she's just a little slow tonight." He led Ethan into the living room. "Take off your coat."

Ethan draped his coat over the back of an armchair.

"Nice shirt," Chris commented, staring at Ethan's loose-fitting silky, red-and-gold-patterned shirt. "Did somebody puke on it?"

"Ha-ha," Ethan replied, frowning. "We're going to that new dance club. You know — the one on the river? It's called River Club."

"Dumb name," Chris said, pulling a handful of cashews from a glass bowl on the coffee table. He pushed the bowl toward Ethan.

"Thanks," Ethan said, tossing several cashews into his mouth. "I didn't get any dinner tonight."

Chris glanced at the clock on the mantel. "You're early, man."

"I know," Ethan replied, grabbing another handful of cashews. "I wasn't sure what time Karen wanted me to pick her up. I was trying to call, but your Call Waiting is messed up."

"Huh?" Chris had started to drop some cashews into his mouth, but stopped.

"Your Call Waiting — it's messed up," Ethan said. "I kept getting a busy signal. I couldn't get through."

Chris lowered his hand with the cashews still in it and eyed Ethan suspiciously. "What are you talking about, Ethan?" he exclaimed, his expression puzzled. "We don't *have* Call Waiting."

Chapter 19

Karen made her way down the stairs a few minutes later. She wore a silky yellow blouse tucked into a very short suede skirt over dark green tights. "Hey, I'm ready!" she called cheerfully.

She stopped at the bottom of the stairs, surprised to see Chris, Ethan, and her mother huddled together on the living room couch. They were talking in hushed tones. They instantly stopped and stared at Karen as she entered the doorway.

"What's up?" she demanded brightly, flashing Ethan a smile.

Her smile faded as the three on the couch continued to stare across the living room at her.

"What's the problem? Is my skirt on backwards or something?" Karen asked with a short giggle. She moved into the room, studying their faces.

Her mother climbed to her feet. She chewed her lower lip. "Karen, Ethan and your brother have just told me a disturbing story. About Call Waiting."

"Huh?" Karen didn't catch on at first. "Call Waiting?"

"We don't *have* Call Waiting," Chris said vehemently. "You pretended — "

"Oh!" Karen cried out as she began to realize what they were talking about.

"Be quiet, Chris," Mrs. Masters said sharply. "Let me talk to her."

Karen could feel her face growing hot. She knew she must be red as a beet. She turned her gaze on Ethan. He avoided her eyes and appeared to shrink into the couch.

"What's the story with these frightening phone calls?" Mrs. Masters demanded, her hands clasped tensely in front of her.

"Well — " Karen took a deep breath.

"You told Ethan someone made threatening calls to you," her mother continued, her dark eyes burning into Karen's, as if searching for answers inside Karen's brain. "Each time, Ethan was on the line."

Mrs. Masters glanced back at Ethan. "Is that right?"

Ethan nodded uncomfortably and appeared to shrink even deeper into the couch.

"You told Ethan you had Call Waiting," Mrs. Masters accused. "But we don't have it, Karen. So how did you get these frightening phone calls?"

Her mother stared even harder at her, leaning forward tensely, her hands pressed firmly against her waist.

Chris shook his head, a tight frown on his face.

Ethan trained his eyes on Karen. She could see hurt and confusion in them.

"Okay, okay," she sighed, in a low voice just above a whisper. "Okay, okay."

She dropped heavily into the armchair across from the couch. Her shoulders were slumped. She lowered her head so she wouldn't have to face their staring eyes.

"Karen, how did you get the frightening calls?" her mother demanded softly.

"I didn't," Karen muttered.

"What?" Mrs. Masters asked.

"I didn't get any calls," Karen told them. "I made them all up."

Chapter 20

"I didn't get any calls. I only pretended," Karen said softly. She brushed a lock of dark hair off her forehead with a trembling hand.

"This is so . . . embarrassing," she murmured, keeping her eyes lowered, feeling her neck muscles tense.

"But why, Karen?" Mrs. Masters demanded. "Why on earth would you do such a thing?"

"You always say *my* jokes are the dumbest!" Chris exclaimed, shaking his head. "Well, this is the dumbest thing I ever heard of!"

"Chris — please!" Mrs. Masters scolded sharply. "Give your sister a chance to talk. This isn't a joke. It's serious." Her voice caught in her throat. She swallowed hard. And then she added quietly, "It's very serious."

"I really don't want to talk about it," Karen

told them, rubbing the back of her neck. "Chris is right. It was really dumb."

"I'm afraid we *have* to talk about it," her mother said. She crossed over to Karen and put a gentle hand on her shoulder. "I don't want to embarrass you, dear. I want to help you. I need to know why you thought you had to invent those frightening calls."

"To keep Ethan!" Karen blurted out shrilly. She felt tears glaze over her eyes. She sucked in her breath and held it, willing herself not to cry.

She felt her mother's hand squeeze her shoulder tenderly. "I don't understand," Mrs. Masters said, her voice barely above a whisper.

Two hot tears rolled down Karen's cheeks. She brushed them away with her fingers. "Ethan was going to break up with me. To go out with Wendy," she said, avoiding her mother's reproachful eyes.

"No way!" Ethan protested, pulling himself to the edge of the couch. "No way, Karen. That just isn't true."

"I . . . I made up the calls so he'd . . . stay with me," Karen reluctantly choked out. She raised her eyes, a pleading expression on her face. "Oh, Mom — this is so embarrassing!

Can't I just go to the dance club now?"

Mrs. Masters ran her hand through Karen's hair. Karen pulled her head away. "Can't Ethan and I go now?" she pleaded shrilly. "I've confessed, okay? I admit I was a jerk. So can I go now?"

"It's sick," she heard Chris mutter from the couch. "It's really sick."

"Shut up, Chris!" Karen snapped.

"Karen — " her mother said sharply. "You don't seem to understand how serious this is. You — "

"Yes I do!" Karen interrupted, jumping to her feet. "Yes, I do! But I said I'm sorry, okay? Haven't I been embarrassed enough for one night? Haven't I?"

"You don't need to be embarrassed," Mrs. Masters said softly, her dark eyes studying Karen with concern. "We all care about you, dear. I — I'm going to get you the help you need."

"Help? What do you mean *help*?" Karen screamed. She could feel herself losing control now. But she couldn't help it. Why was her mother talking about *help*? "I did a dumb thing, that's all," Karen muttered.

"But it's important to understand why," Mrs. Masters insisted.

"You mean you want to send me to a

shrink?" Karen cried, squeezing her hands tightly around her waist, staring angrily at her mother.

"Adam went to a very good doctor in town," Mrs. Masters said thoughtfully. "Before his family moved. He was upset about the move, and this doctor talked to him and helped him a lot. I'll call over there and get the doctor's name."

"Mother, I don't need a shrink," Karen uttered through clenched teeth.

"It wouldn't hurt to talk to someone," Mrs. Masters said.

"You're nuts!" Chris declared, stretching his arms above his head. "Totally nuts."

"Chris — I'm warning you!" Mrs. Masters cried angrily. "You're supposed to be the man in the family. Instead, you're acting like a two-year-old."

"Hey, *I'm* not the one who's nuts!" Chris protested.

Ethan was leaning forward on the couch, hands clasped tensely in front of him, staring toward the doorway.

"Can I go to the dance club or not?" Karen demanded, staring furiously at her mother.

Mrs. Masters hesitated, biting her lower lip. "Only if you promise you'll talk to the doctor," she said finally.

"Okay, okay," Karen muttered grudgingly. She turned to Ethan. "Let's go, okay?"

Ethan climbed to his feet. He had bright pink circles on his cheeks. He avoided her glance. Karen could see that he was totally embarrassed.

I've really blown it this time, Karen thought miserably.

Everyone thinks I'm a nut case. Ethan, too. He'll definitely break up with me now. Why should he hang around with a nut case?

Pretending to get the scary calls had seemed like a harmless way to keep Ethan interested in her. When she had seen him talking with Wendy, laughing with Wendy, standing so close to Wendy, Karen had realized that she would do *anything* to hold on to Ethan.

Anything.

But now her desperate plan had backfired. If only she hadn't been caught. . . .

Ethan followed her to the front closet. Silently, he helped her on with her coat.

He's staring at me as if I'm some kind of sicko, Karen thought miserably. Ethan thinks I'm a nut case.

"Not too late!" Mrs. Masters called from the living room.

"Don't wait up!" Karen called back. She

forced a smile at Ethan, but he didn't smile back.

They stepped out into the windy, cold night. The seats in the red Bonneville were cold. Karen could feel the cold even through her skirt and tights.

Ethan drove to the club in silence, his eyes straight ahead on the road, a thoughtful expression on his face.

"I — I'm really sorry about . . . everything," Karen offered, putting her hand on his.

"It's okay," he replied without looking at her.

She forced a laugh. "It's actually kind of funny, don't you think?"

He hesitated. "I guess," he replied.

At the River Club, Ethan seemed to cheer up a little. They began to dance as soon as they arrived, moving to the loud, throbbing rhythms under flashing red-and-blue lights.

Karen was beginning to feel better, just starting to relax, when Ethan led her to the tables at the side of the dance floor. "I'll be right back," he told her, shouting over the pounding music.

Before Karen could protest, he disappeared toward the front of the club.

Where is he going in such a hurry? Karen

wondered. She stood uncomfortably against
the wall, watching the red-and-blue forms of
the swaying, bobbing dancers under the swirl
of lights.

When Ethan hadn't returned five minutes
later, Karen took a seat at one of the tiny
tables. Elbows on the table, she rested her
head in her hands, her eyes searching eagerly
for Ethan.

Where is he? What can he be doing?

She jumped up as a frightening thought
flashed into her mind: Has he left me here?

No. Of course not, she assured herself.

There I go being crazy again.

She decided to follow him. She made her
way across the dance floor, pushing and bump-
ing her way through the dancing couples.

They all seem so happy, she thought. Why
can't Ethan and I be happy, too?

She stopped when she saw him. He was
leaning against the wall, talking into a pay
phone, a hand over his free ear, trying to block
out the loud music.

Who can he be talking to now? she wondered, feeling her neck muscles tighten.

Ethan glanced up and saw Karen. He gave
her a quick wave, then turned his back as he
continued his call.

Karen stood at the edge of the dance floor.

The red-and-blue lights swirled over her. The floor appeared to tilt and sway in time to the steady, relentless rhythm.

She shut her eyes, but the flashing, rolling colors didn't go away.

When she opened her eyes, Ethan was standing in front of her.

"Did you just call Wendy?" The words burst out of her.

"Huh?" He swept a hand back through his long hair and leaned forward to hear her over the music.

"Did you just call Wendy?" Karen repeated, shouting into his ear.

"No way," Ethan replied, frowning.

"Swear to me you're not going out with Wendy!" Karen cried.

"Huh? I can't hear!" He brought his face close to hers. His long hair brushed her cheek.

"Swear to me!" Karen screamed. "Swear to me you're not interested in Wendy!"

Ethan solemnly raised a hand as if taking an oath. "I swear it," he shouted.

Did she believe him?

She wasn't sure.

As they began to dance, a slow, soft dance, she held on to Ethan so tightly, so tightly, he couldn't get away if he wanted to.

* * *

Nearly two weeks later, on a snowy Thursday night, Ethan arrived at Karen's house after dinner for a study date. Mrs. Masters greeted him at the front door and ushered him inside.

"Is the snow sticking?" she asked, peering over his shoulder as Ethan stamped his wet boots on the rubber floor mat.

"It's starting to," he told her. He brushed some wet snowflakes from his long, black hair.

"Before you go up to study with Karen, I want to thank you," Mrs. Masters said quietly.

"Huh? Thank me?" Ethan reacted with surprise. He pulled off his backpack and followed her away from the front stairs.

"You've been so considerate," Mrs. Masters whispered, glancing to the stairs, not wanting Karen to hear. "You've been so attentive to Karen. I really appreciate it, Ethan."

Pink circles formed on his cheeks. He shook his head hard as if trying to shake away the compliment.

"It's been so good of you to come over every night and to see Karen every weekend," Mrs. Masters continued, not noticing his embarrassment. "You've really been so good for her. You have no idea. You really have made the difference, seeing her through this bad time."

"That's good," Ethan replied awkwardly. "I'm glad."

"Dr. Rudman says that he's had some very good sessions with Karen," Mrs. Masters continued, shoving her hands into her jeans pockets. "He says he's very encouraged by Karen's progress."

"Great," Ethan murmured.

"Well, I didn't mean to embarrass you," Mrs. Masters said, smiling warmly at him. "I just wanted to thank you for being there for Karen. Go on upstairs."

"Okay. Thanks," Ethan replied. Hoisting his backpack over one shoulder, he eagerly made his way up to Karen's room.

She glanced up from the open book on her desk as he entered. "What were you and Mom talking about?" she demanded.

"Nothing much. Just the weather," Ethan told her.

Karen started to say something, but the telephone rang. She picked up the receiver after the first ring. "Hello?"

"Karen, this is your imagination calling," a harsh, throaty voice whispered in her ear. *"I'm inside your brain. I'm going to kill you. I'm really going to kill you."*

Chapter 21

"No!" Karen screamed.

The phone dropped from her hand, clattering onto the desk.

"What *is* it?" Ethan demanded, his eyes wide with surprise.

"It's real!" Karen choked out. "Ethan, it's real this time! The call — "

He grabbed the receiver. "Let me hear!" He raised it to his ear. "Hello? Hello? Who's there?"

Karen stared at him as he listened intently. He turned to her, a bewildered expression on his face. "Just a dial tone," he murmured. He replaced the receiver.

Karen threw her arms around him and pressed her face against his chest. "It was so horrible, Ethan! Such an ugly, raspy voice. He said he was my imagination. He said he was inside my brain and he was going to kill me!"

Ethan didn't reply.

Karen pulled back and studied his face. "You believe me — don't you?"

"Yeah. Of course," Ethan replied automatically.

Karen caught the doubt in his eyes.

He doesn't believe me.

Ethan doesn't believe me.

She shoved him angrily away with both fists. "It's real this time!" she cried. "It was a real call, Ethan!"

"I believe you," he insisted. "Really, Karen. I believe you."

But she could see in his eyes that he didn't. She could see in his tight-lipped expression that he thought she was inventing another drama.

Late that night, Karen lay wide awake, unable to fall asleep, staring at the rectangle of light on her ceiling from the streetlight outside her bedroom window.

The whispered voice repeated its harsh threat in her mind again and again. *"I'm inside your brain. I'm going to kill you. I'm really going to kill you."*

Ethan didn't believe me, she thought
miserably.

He had made an excuse and hurried home.

He didn't believe me. Even though this time
it was real.

Real. Real. Real.

Was someone *really* going to kill her?

She shut her eyes, trying to force the harsh
whisper from her mind, trying to will herself
asleep.

When she reopened her eyes, she became
aware of darting shadows.

Movement. The creak of the floorboards.

A nearly silent footstep.

Someone is here, Karen realized. Someone
is in my room.

She struggled to sit up, but was held down
by a hidden force, a heavy weight.

Paralyzed. I'm paralyzed.

What is happening to me? Why can't I sit
up?

The floorboards groaned again, closer this
time to her bed.

Shadows bent and shifted.

She stared into the darkness, still struggling
to sit up.

But the heavy weight pressed against her
chest, held her head flat on the pillow. Her
hair felt wet and sticky under her head.

Shadows moved.

She heard a muffled cough.

"*I'm inside your brain. I'm going to kill you. I'm really going to kill you.*"

Black shadows slid over gray shadows.

The floorboards creaked and groaned.

"Who — who's there?" Karen's voice came out harsh and raspy. *She had the same voice as the caller on the phone!*

"Who's in my room?" she called in the throaty whisper.

Silence. Sliding shadows close to the bed.

And then a figure moved out of the shadows. And a face lowered itself right above hers.

"Chris!" Karen cried.

He grinned down at her, his face half in shadow, half in light.

"Chris — what are you doing in my room?" she cried.

His face floated over hers. His grin grew wider. His eyes burned down into hers. "It isn't a joke," he said.

"Huh? Chris? What do you want?" Karen cried.

"It isn't a joke," Chris repeated.

And then Karen saw the gleaming blade — and recognized the big kitchen knife her brother raised slowly in his hand.

Chapter 22

"Chris — please!" Karen pleaded.

The knife blade gleamed, lowering toward her throat.

If only she could move. If only she could sit up, slide away.

But the weight pressed down on her, holding her there beneath the gleaming blade, beneath her brother's frightening, unwavering grin.

"Chris — ?"

He backed away suddenly, his face fading into the shadows.

And Karen suddenly realized to her horror that he wasn't alone. Shadows moved silently. Other faces appeared.

"Adam!" she whispered. "Adam — are you here, too?"

Beside Adam she saw Ethan. Then Jake. She saw Micah's tangles of blonde hair next, and then Micah was there. Chris, and Adam, and Ethan, and Jake, and Micah — and Wendy!

Their faces were illuminated by a silvery glow. The glow of broad knife blades.

They all held kitchen knives. The gleaming blades rose above Karen, shining brighter and brighter, until she had to turn away, had to shut her eyes from the shimmering white glare.

"Have you *all* come to kill me?" she wondered.

"It isn't a joke," Chris said. "It isn't a joke this time."

No. It's a dream, Karen suddenly knew.

She knew when she opened her eyes, the faces, the knives, the shadows would all be gone.

Just a dream. A frightening dream, she told herself.

She opened her eyes.

She sat up.

She had been right. She stared into the silent darkness.

Just a horrible dream.

She stared at the ceiling for the rest of the night, afraid the dream might continue if she fell back to sleep.

*   *   *

A few days later, Ethan met her outside the lunchroom in school. "How's it going?" he asked cheerfully. "Did you ace Carver's midterm?"

"Think so," Karen replied, bending down to pick up a penny. "Hey, look what I found. Isn't finding a penny supposed to be good luck?"

Ethan had turned away, she realized. Tucking the penny into her jeans pocket, she saw that Jake had appeared.

"Where've you been, man?" Jake demanded in his raspy voice, after slapping Ethan a high-five in greeting. "I haven't seen you in days."

Ethan's cheeks turned pink. "Well, I've been spending a lot of time with Karen," he explained.

Karen turned to see Jake glaring at her coldly.

Jake doesn't like me! Karen suddenly realized. The discovery caught her by surprise. She had known Jake even longer than she had known Ethan.

But until this moment, she had never realized that Jake didn't like her.

"You want to grab some lunch?" Jake asked Ethan.

Ethan turned to Karen. "No. Not today. Karen and I — "

"Okay. Later," Jake said, shrugging. He

shambled away, his long grasshopper legs taking unhurried strides.

"If you'd rather have lunch with Jake — " Karen started.

Ethan shook his head. "No. Come on. Did you bring your lunch, or do you want to buy something?"

Before Karen could answer, she felt someone tap the back of her sweater. She turned around to see Jessica Forrest, a girl she knew.

"Karen, there's a call for you," Jessica informed her. "In the principal's office."

"Huh? A call? Who is it?" Karen demanded.

Jessica shook her head. "I don't know. I work in the office at lunchtime. They just told me to try to find you."

Karen felt her heart start to thud in her chest. Blood pulsed at her temples.

Who would call her at the office? Was something wrong with her mom? Was there an accident? Had something terrible happened?

"I'll save you a seat," Ethan said, pointing to the lunchroom.

Karen barely heard him. Her mind whirring with frightening thoughts of what the call could be, she followed Jessica to the office, half-walking, half-jogging.

Jessica stopped to talk to some kids. Karen hurried past her.

She ran into the principal's office and breath-lessly grabbed up the phone at the end of the long counter. "Hello?"

"I can see you, Karen," the throaty voice rasped into her ear. *"I'm in your mind. I'm your worst nightmare. I'm going to kill you."*

Karen's mouth dropped open, but no sound came out.

The phone receiver trembled in her hand.

Who is doing this to me? she asked herself.

Do they just want to frighten me? Or do they really plan to kill me?

Who is it? *Who?*

She tried again to say something. But the phone had gone dead.

The dial tone buzzed in her ear.

"Don't use that phone," a woman's voice called.

"Huh?" Karen dropped the receiver onto the phone.

"Don't use that phone, Karen."

Karen turned, her heart pounding, to see Mrs. Ferguson, the office secretary, pointing at her. "Huh? What's wrong, Mrs. Ferguson?" Karen asked in a quivering voice.

"You'll have to use a different phone," Mrs. Ferguson instructed. "That phone isn't work-ing at all, Karen. It's out of order."

Chapter 23

How can the phone be broken? Karen asked herself, staring hard at it. I just heard that frightening voice. He talked to me on that phone!

I didn't imagine it! I *didn't*! Karen told herself.

With a cry of despair, she turned and bolted from the office. She could hear Mrs. Ferguson's alarmed voice calling after her. But Karen ignored it and kept running.

Out into the crowded hall, filled with kids returning from lunch, getting ready for fifth-period classes. Karen turned first left, then right, unsure of where she wanted to go — and stumbled right into Adam.

"Hey — !" he cried out, startled, and dropped his brown leather briefcase on his foot.

"Adam?" His surprised face blurred in front

of her. The floor appeared to rise up beneath
her. Karen backed up against the wall, breathing hard, and waited for her head to clear.
"Adam, what are you doing here?"

"I go to school here, remember?" he shot
back, staring at her hard through his black-
framed glasses. "What's your problem,
Karen? You look terrible!"

"I — don't feel well," she told him, rubbing
her throbbing temples with both hands. "I
really feel sick, I think."

"I have my mom's car," Adam said, leaning
toward her, trying to make himself heard over
the slamming lockers and shouting voices.
"Want me to drive you home?"

"Uh . . . yeah," Karen replied impulsively.
"Thanks, Adam. I really do feel sick." She
glanced up at him, trying to make his face come
into focus. But it remained a fuzzy blur. "Won't
you get into trouble?"

He shook his head. "I'll drive you home and
be back in five minutes. I only have study hall
next period, anyway."

Karen made her way unsteadily down the
hall to her locker, where she collected her coat
and books. Then she hurried out to the student
parking lot.

A few seconds later, she was sitting next
to Adam in his mother's old Honda Civic. It

was a wet, gray day. Most of the snow had melted, but a few large patches dotted the ground.

The tires spun on a small square of ice as Adam pulled out of the student parking lot. He was tapping the wheel with both hands, nervously rapping out a rapid rhythm.

"Feeling any better?" he asked, eyes straight ahead on the road.

"A little," Karen replied, pressing her hot forehead against the cool window. "I have to call Dr. Rudman."

Adam thought about her answer for a while before replying. "What's the problem?"

"Phone calls," Karen said under her breath. "I — I've been getting these horrible, threatening calls. For real."

Adam didn't react. He turned onto Fairfield.

"I just got a call. In the office. This frightening voice. I don't know who it could be. He said he could see me. He said he was going to kill me."

Adam glanced over at her, then quickly returned his eyes to the windshield.

"But then Mrs. Ferguson said the phone was out of order, that it wasn't working," Karen continued with a sigh.

Adam hummed under his breath. "Wow."

"You don't believe me, do you?" Karen accused.

"Well . . ."

"No one believes me," Karen said angrily. "You think I'm crazy, don't you, Adam."

"No. Of course not," he replied.

"I'm not making up these calls," Karen told him. "I'm not. They're real. Someone is really trying to scare me. I made up the other calls. I admit that. It was a really stupid thing to do. But these calls are real, Adam."

"On a busted phone?" Adam exclaimed.

Karen sank back in her seat.

Adam thinks I'm crazy. He thinks I'm hallucinating or hearing things or something.

I'm not. I'm not!

She realized she was desperately trying to convince *herself*!

"Well, as soon as I get home, I'm going to call Dr. Rudman," she said, more to herself than to Adam.

"Good idea," Adam muttered.

"Why are we stopping?" Karen cried, suddenly frightened. She stared hard at her cousin.

"Because you're home," he replied, gesturing out the window.

"Oh!" Karen could feel her cheeks growing red. "Sorry. I really am a basket case today."

She pushed open the car door. "Thanks for the lift, Adam. I really appreciate it."

"Hope you're okay," Adam said.

"You don't believe me — do you!" Karen blurted out, suddenly feeling very sorry for herself. "You think I'm making up these calls."

Adam shrugged his slender shoulders. "I don't know, Karen." And then his eyes narrowed behind his glasses as he added, "Sometimes I hear voices, too."

"Adam — "

"Sometimes I hear them late at night," he continued, his expression solemn.

"Adam, please — " Karen pleaded. "I'd better get inside, okay? Thanks again." She climbed out and slammed the door shut behind her.

He's totally weird, she thought as she ran around to the back door. Totally weird.

Karen let herself into the house. The kitchen smelled of stale eggs and bacon. The breakfast dishes were still in the sink.

"Anybody home?" she called.

Of course not. Chris was at school. Her mother was at work.

She let her backpack fall to the floor, crossed the room to the refrigerator, and pulled out a can of Coke.

It felt strange being home in the middle of

the day, walking through the silent, empty
house. She felt like an intruder. She felt as if
she didn't belong here.

Crazy thoughts.

I'd better call Dr. Rudman, she thought
unhappily.

As she started toward the kitchen phone on
the wall, it rang.

The sound burst through the heavy silence.

Startled, Karen nearly dropped the Coke
can.

A second ring.

She stood frozen in the center of the floor,
staring in horror at the red wallphone.

Was it the frightening caller?

Was he really watching her? Had he followed
her home?

Should she answer it?

Chapter 24

After the third ring, Karen grabbed the receiver and pressed it to her ear. "Hello?" Her voice came out tight and frightened.

"Karen? You went home?"

"Ethan!" she exclaimed, sighing with relief. "Ethan, I'm sorry. I — "

"I waited for you," he said. "By the lunchroom. What happened?"

Karen could hear loud voices in the background. She heard lockers slamming, kids laughing. She knew Ethan was using the pay phone outside the library.

"I — I got another call," she stammered into the phone. "It was really frightening, Ethan. The same hoarse voice. He said he was going to kill me."

"That's terrible," Ethan murmured without any feeling.

"You don't believe me — do you!" Karen

accused, her voice trembling. "It was a real call, Ethan. A real threat. Do you believe me? *Do* you?"

He didn't reply.

The kids' voices in the background seemed to grow louder.

She heard a long bell ring.

"I've got to go," Ethan told her. "That's the bell. I was worried about you, so — "

"But do you believe me?" Karen demanded, not intending to sound so desperate.

"I'll call you later. I've got to run," he said. "Call Dr. Rudman, okay?"

He hung up.

Karen remained with the phone pressed to her ear, leaning against the kitchen wall, the steady buzz of the dial tone drilling into her brain.

He thinks I'm making it up, she thought bitterly.

The next morning Karen dreaded returning to school. Would the kids be gossiping about her? Would word have gotten around that she had left school in the middle of the day because she was hearing weird voices on broken phones?

Her mind whirring with troubled thoughts, Karen was halfway down the driveway when she realized she had forgotten her coat.

"I really *am* losing it!" she said out loud, hurrying back to the house.

She arrived at school a few minutes before the final bell and hurried to the office to deliver the absence excuse note her mom had written.

The two secretaries were arguing about pencils as Karen stepped up to the long counter. "The Number Two pencil is softer than the Number Three," Mrs. Ferguson was insisting.

"They're not numbered for softness," the other secretary insisted. "They're numbered for darkness."

"Mrs. Ferguson?" Karen called, holding the folded-up excuse note over the counter. "Sorry to interrupt — "

Mrs. Ferguson made her way to the counter. "Good morning, Karen."

"My absence excuse," Karen muttered, handing her the note.

Mrs. Ferguson unfolded the note and glanced at it quickly. Then she raised her eyes to Karen. "I owe you an apology," she said, folding the note up again.

"Huh? For what?"

"For yesterday," Mrs. Ferguson replied. She pointed to the phone at the end of the counter. "The phone *wasn't* out of order. It had been broken for three days. But the guy came to fix it yesterday morning, and nobody told me." She smiled at Karen. "Sorry."

"Uh . . . that's okay," Karen replied.

The bell rang. Karen turned and hurried out the door.

So the phone had been working after all.

Knowing that fact didn't cheer her up at all.

That only meant one thing: *The call was real!*

The threat was real.

Someone who knows me is trying to scare me, Karen realized.

Someone wants to scare me — or kill me!

But who?

The halls were empty. She was late.

Her footsteps echoed in the long, silent hall. A classroom door slammed hard, startling her.

She turned a corner, heading to her locker to deposit her coat — and someone grabbed her from behind.

Chapter 25

Karen cried out, her voice echoing down the long, empty hall.

An evil laugh invaded her ears.

She spun around. "Chris! You creep!"

Her brother grinned at her, pleased that he had scared her.

"Chris — what are you *doing* here?" she cried angrily.

"Thought you might need this," he said, still grinning. He held up her backpack.

"Oh, no," Karen moaned. "I left without my coat this morning. Did I forget that, too?" She grabbed the backpack away from him.

"Getting a teensy bit absentminded, are we?" he teased.

"Thanks for bringing it," Karen said. Then she added,"You didn't have to scare me to death."

"Why not?" he replied, laughing. He gave

her a quick wave, then headed toward the exit.

Karen stood watching him leave, shaking her head.

Why does he enjoy scaring me so much? He really never misses an opportunity. . . .

A door slammed, stirring her from her thoughts.

She dropped her coat in her locker and, lugging the backpack on one shoulder, ran down the hall to homeroom.

Karen slipped her hands around Ethan's neck and pulled his face close.

They kissed. A long, sweet kiss.

She moved her hands up to his long black hair and stroked his head as she kissed him.

When the kiss ended, she sighed breathlessly and lowered her forehead to his chest.

They sat in silence for a long while.

I've never felt so close to him, Karen thought happily.

She snuggled against him, wondering what he was thinking.

They were at one end of the den couch. A single lamp cast an orange glow over the room.

Wish we had a fireplace, Karen thought dreamily.

She raised her face for another kiss. But Ethan climbed quickly to his feet.

"Where are you going?" she asked, surprised.

"Jake's," Ethan muttered. "I told him I'd
come over." He glanced across the room to
the desk clock.

"Jake's? How come you're spending so
much time with Jake these days?" Karen demanded, unable to keep the hurt from her
voice.

"He's my friend — remember?" Ethan replied sharply.

Karen jumped up and threw her arms
around Ethan's waist. She hugged him, pressing her face against his long, soft hair. "Don't
go," she whispered.

Ethan turned to face her, gently removing
her arms from around him. "I promised Jake.
Really."

"I — I really don't feel like being alone here
tonight," Karen said shakily.

"Sorry," he replied, lowering his eyes.

"Can I call you at Jake's?" she asked.

He hesitated. "Well . . . we might go out."

"Ethan — do you believe me about the
phone calls?" The words tumbled from her
mouth. She hadn't planned to talk about the
calls. But the fact that Ethan doubted her had
been troubling her mind the entire evening.

"Um . . . yeah," he replied, tugging at the

tiny silver ring in his earlobe. "I do."

Karen wasn't sure she believed him.

"Do you have any idea who might be making the calls?" she asked.

He started toward the front door. "Some creep, I guess," he replied.

"Some creep?" She followed him across the living room.

Halfway to the door, he turned back to her. "What makes you think it's someone we know?" he demanded. "It's probably a total stranger, Karen. You know. Someone who just punched your number at random."

"No," she insisted, crossing her arms over the front of her purple sweater. "No. No way. Whoever it is knows my name, Ethan. They didn't dial it at random. They reached me at school, remember? They asked for me at school. They *know* me, Ethan."

"Yeah. I guess you're right," he said softly. He picked up his jacket from the stairway. "Call me if you need me," he told her.

She came forward to give him a good-night kiss. But he hurried out the door.

Upstairs in her room, Karen tried to study. But the words in the government text became a dark blur on the page.

I feel so alone, Karen thought, bent over

the desk, supporting her chin on her fists. I really need a friend.

Maybe it's time I made up with Micah, she told herself.

Actually, Dr. Rudman had suggested it.

She and Micah had been close friends all year. They had so much in common. They had always been able to talk about their problems together.

"Micah." Karen said her name out loud. "Micah. Micah." Such a pretty name.

She glanced at the desk clock. Almost ten. Not too late to call.

I'll phone her and apologize, Karen decided.

But before she could reach for the phone, it rang.

She reached across the desk and picked it up before the first ring had ended. "Hello?"

"This is your imagination, Karen."

The hoarse, whispered voice in her ear.

"I'm inside your brain. Can you feel me in there?"

"No!" Karen cried angrily. "Leave me alone! Leave me alone! Do you hear me?"

"But I'm inside your brain, Karen," the frightening voice rasped. *"I can't leave you alone. I'm going to kill you. Maybe tonight!"*

Karen started to cry out again — but she muffled herself when she heard a sound.

A sound behind the rasping voice.

One sound.

Karen listened to the sound. Heard it again clearly.

And knew who the caller was.

Chapter 26

Her heart pounding, Karen grabbed her coat and hurried out to the car. It was a clear, cold night. A pale half-moon shimmered in a dark purple sky. Small patches of snow dotted the dark ground.

The blue Corolla started easily. But the windshield was frosted over with a thin layer of ice.

Karen impatiently tried brushing it away with the wipers, but it didn't work. With a loud groan, she climbed out of the car and scraped the windshield with a plastic scraper.

"I hate winter!" she cried aloud.

Tossing the scraper onto the back seat, she climbed back into the car, switched on the headlights, and headed away.

I can't believe this, she thought.

I really can't believe this.

But she knew she was right. She knew who

had been calling her. She knew who had been threatening her, frightening her.

Now she had to find out *why*.

Her foot pressed down all the way on the gas pedal, Karen drove through a stop sign without even noticing.

"I can't believe that someone so close to me would do that!" she cried aloud.

She suddenly realized she was gripping the wheel so tightly, her hands ached.

With a furious cry, she made a sharp turn onto Jefferson.

Most of the houses were already dark, she saw, even though it was only ten-fifteen.

The houses, the front yards, the winter-bare trees rolled past the window in a dark blur.

A few moments later, from the top of the hill where she had spied on him, Ethan's low, ranch-style house came into view.

Feeling her anger rise in her chest, Karen lowered her foot on the brake to slow the car.

Chapter 27

Karen stared out at Ethan's house, stretching darkly over the flat lawn.

The car slowed nearly to a halt. She realized her legs were trembling.

Her entire body was shaking.

Shaking with anger. With hurt.

How could somebody so close to me want to frighten me like that?

It was a question she knew she had to answer.

The light was on in Ethan's bedroom in the far corner of the house.

Is he home from Jake's already? Karen wondered. Is he in there right now?

Ethan. Ethan. Ethan. The name repeated in her mind.

But the horrifying question pushed Ethan's name aside:

How could somebody so close to me want to frighten me like that?

Taking a deep breath and holding it, Karen drove the car past Ethan's house. Past the house next to it. Past the empty lot beside that.

Then she made a sharp right turn into the long driveway across the street.

The wide yard was still covered by a thin layer of snow. A light over the porch cast pale white light over the gray-shingled front of the house.

The bare trees shifted in a slight wind. What were they whispering to her? Karen wondered.

Were they telling her to go back?

Karen closed the car door quietly behind her and then raced up to the front door.

What am I doing here? she asked herself, running on trembling legs.

What am I going to do?

What am I going to say?

She leaned against the glass storm door, pressing both hands against the glass, struggling to catch her breath.

The front door, she saw, was open a crack. A line of bright yellow light seeped through the opening.

She grabbed the handle of the storm door and pulled the door open.

She listened.

Silence.

Behind her on the street, a car rumbled past.

Karen pushed open the wooden front door just wide enough to slip inside.

Now what?

What do I say? What do I do?

The living room was brightly lit. A fire crackled in the fireplace. All of the lamps were on. The chrome-and-white-leather couches appeared to glow in the bright light.

An enormous, framed movie poster of Clark Gable and Vivien Leigh from *Gone With the Wind* hung on the wall opposite the window.

Karen had always loved that poster, loved the strength of Clark Gable as he carried Vivien Leigh up the tall staircase.

But now it filled her with revulsion.

She hated the poster, hated the modern white couches and chairs, hated the room, the whole house.

Why am I here?

What will I say? What will I do?

Karen gasped and froze against the wall as Micah came into view.

Micah had her back to Karen. She was

dressed in loose-fitting gray sweats.

She sat on a square, white leather ottoman in front of the window. One hand held a cordless phone to her ear. The other hand toyed with strands of her thick, blonde hair.

Her back pressed against the wall, her knees shaking so hard she could barely stand, Karen stared across the brightly lit room at her old friend.

What should I say to her?

What should I do?

"Micah — !" Karen screamed before she even realized it. "Micah — I know it's you!"

Micah gasped and dropped the phone to the plush white carpet. She jumped up unsteadily from the ottoman, her green eyes wide with shock.

"How did you get in?" Micah cried.

Karen stepped toward her. "I know it was you!" she repeated in a tight, angry voice she didn't recognize. "Why, Micah? Why did you do that to me?"

"Huh? How do you know it was me?" Micah snapped back, her shocked expression turning to anger. "How do you know, Karen?"

"Oh, Micah," Karen sobbed. "I heard the chimes. It was ten o'clock. I heard the stupid chimes behind your whispering voice."

Micah's mouth dropped open, but no sound came out.

"Oops." Micah shrugged. Her expression remained hard, her eyes trained warily on Karen.

"Why?" Karen demanded again, taking a few steps closer. "Tell me why."

Micah backed toward the fire, her hands tensed at her sides. "You're so dumb, Karen," she murmured scornfully.

"No name-calling," Karen said sharply. "Just explain, Micah. Just explain why."

"For Ethan, of course," Micah replied with a sneer. She tossed her hair behind her shoulder with one hand.

"Huh? Ethan?"

Micah let out a scornful laugh. "You mean you didn't *know* about Ethan and me? You didn't know that Ethan planned to break up with you so that he and I — "

"But I thought it was Wendy — " Karen interrupted.

Micah shook her head. "He was never interested in Wendy," she said softly. She picked up the iron poker from its stand and turned to jab at the fire. "Why do you think I was spending so much time with Jake, Karen? So that I could see Ethan. Ethan and I met at

Jake's. You couldn't possibly think I was interested in Jake — could you?"

"I — I didn't know," Karen replied weakly.

"But you ruined it. You ruined everything," Micah said with emotion, poking harder at the fire.

"Ruined it?"

"With those stupid phone calls you made up," Micah said bitterly, her green eyes glowing angrily in the darting orange firelight.

"But, Micah — " Karen started.

"Shut up!" Micah screamed. "You ruined everything. When you started the routine with the phone calls, Ethan suddenly felt so sorry for you, so guilty. He couldn't bring himself to break up with you in your hour of need."

"I know — " Karen said.

But again Micah cut her off. "Shut up, I said! Shut up, Karen!" Micah poked the fire furiously, sending up waves of sparkling cinders. "When you started inventing those stupid phone calls, I never saw Ethan. He was spending all his time with you. Every night. Every weekend. He felt so sorry for you."

Micah twisted her features in disgust. "And all the while, you were a total fraud, Karen. A total fraud. You made up the calls to hold on to Ethan. You ruined everything for me! Everything!"

"But, Micah — you were my friend!" Karen protested breathlessly. "You were supposed to be my *friend*!"

"I tried to warn you," Micah told her. "I came to your house. I tried to warn you that Ethan wasn't worth it." She shook her head bitterly. "But of course you wouldn't listen to me."

"And then you started making those awful calls?" Karen cried.

"You're crazy, anyway," Micah said coldly. "I figured a few *real* calls would send you over the edge. I wanted Ethan to see how crazy you were. I wanted him to realize that he belongs with me — not you."

"No!" Karen cried, her entire body shuddering. "No! No! No!"

Her anger took over. She couldn't hold it back any longer.

Karen opened her mouth in a loud cry of fury.

Then, before she even realized what she was doing, she was plunging across the room, rushing at Micah, ready to hit her, to tear at her, to *hurt* her.

Micah's eyes went wide. She turned from the fire and raised the hot poker.

Karen tried to stop. But her anger was like

a tidal wave, out of control, pushing her, pushing her, carrying her forward.

"No — please!" Karen cried.

But it was too late.

"Ethan is mine now!" Micah screamed.

And she shoved the burning hot poker
through Karen's heart.

Chapter 28

Karen dropped to her knees as the pain burned through her chest.

It took her a short while to realize that she hadn't been stabbed with the poker.

A hot cinder had leapt from the fire and burned through her sweater.

Micah stood over her with the black iron poker poised in one hand. In the bright firelight, her hair glowed as if aflame.

"Give up, Karen," she muttered, narrowing her eyes in hatred.

"No!" Karen shrieked.

Her anger swept her forward again.

She drove blindly with her arms outstretched and tackled Micah around the knees.

Micah cried out as the poker sailed out of her hand and bounced across the carpet.

Karen pulled her down, and the two girls began wrestling furiously on the floor in front of the fire. Uttering breathless cries, they tugged and punched at each other.

This is crazy! This is crazy! Karen realized as she struggled.

But she couldn't stop herself.

She cried out as Micah slipped out from under her and, panting loudly, climbed to her feet.

Karen reached to tackle her again. But Micah dodged away.

And then Karen saw Micah pick up a heavy white lamp from an end table.

Karen struggled to roll out of the way.

But Micah was too quick.

With an anguished groan, Micah raised the lamp above her, preparing to swing it down on Karen's head.

"Please — " Karen managed to cry out, raising her hands and shutting her eyes.

She waited for the lamp to crash down on her. Waited for the pain.

When it didn't come, Karen opened her eyes — to see Ethan pulling the lamp from Micah's hands.

Micah released the lamp without a struggle and took a step back.

"Ethan!" Karen cried joyfully.

"I'm so glad you're here!" Micah declared, throwing herself into Ethan's arms. She pointed down at Karen. "She — she was going to kill me!"

"No — !" Karen protested, struggling to her feet.

"She's crazy!" Micah told Ethan, still pointing at Karen with one hand and holding on to Ethan with the other. "Karen told me she hears voices, Ethan. She said her voices ordered her to kill me! She's so crazy, Ethan! Karen came here to kill me! Because of her voices! We — we have to help her! We have to get her to a hospital right away!"

"Okay," Ethan said softly.

Chapter 29

"Okay, Micah," Ethan repeated softly. "You can stop lying to me."

"Huh?" Micah's mouth dropped open in surprise. Ethan pushed her away from him and helped Karen to her feet. Then he slipped his arm around Karen's waist, holding her tight.

"She's crazy!" Micah insisted weakly. "She hears voices, Ethan. She — "

"Enough," Ethan said softly. "I heard everything, Micah." He pointed to the cordless phone on the carpet. "I was on the phone with you, remember? You didn't turn it off when Karen came in. I heard your whole conversation. That's why I came running over."

Micah sighed. Her shoulders slumped. The light seemed to fade from her green eyes. "But, Ethan, you and I — ?"

Ethan shook his head. "Micah, didn't it ever occur to you that I stayed with Karen through all this because I *care* about her? Sure, you've been after me to break up with her. And I was tempted for a while. But I came to my senses. I realized how much Karen means to me."

Micah let out an anguished sob of defeat. Then she turned away, her features twisted in sadness and dismay.

The room became silent except for the crackling of the fire.

Karen leaned her head against Ethan's shoulder. She felt his arm tighten around her waist.

"Am I hearing voices now?" she asked. "Or did you really say that?"

"*I'm* hearing voices, telling us to leave," he replied softly. Holding her close, he led her to the door.

About the Author

R.L. STINE is the author of more than three dozen mysteries for young people, all of which have been best-sellers. Recent Scholastic horror titles include *The Baby-Sitter III*, *The Dead Girlfriend*, and *Halloween Night*.

In addition, he is the author of two popular monthly series: *Goosebumps* and *Fear Street*.

Bob lives in New York City with his wife, Jane, and thirteen-year-old son, Matt.

THRILLERS